Own Your Light

Becoming Your Favorite Self So You Can Bring Your Best to the World

STEPHANIE ANN BALL

For Carol Kirkpatrick, the woman
who turned my light back on
and refused to let me blow it out.

May the words in these pages
bring you joy and inspiration!

~ *[signature]*

Contents

Foreword

I'm honored to have been asked to write the foreword to Stephanie Ann Ball's book "Own Your Light". The process of getting to know your authentic, favorite self is one of trial and error and requires risk, bravery, vulnerability, and commitment. That might seem like doing the impossible. But, as you read through her book, it's like Stephanie is actually there, talking you through the necessary steps as you cautiously move forward. You can tell from her writing that she too has gone through this transformation and understands the frustrations and stumbling blocks to look out for. She is truly giving you the tools and skills to light your very own path as you move forward.

This is not a band-aid or quick fix. This is you being responsible for how you get what you want out of life and allowing your light to shine its brightest. As Stephanie says, "I felt that someone, somewhere, needed to hear what I had to say because they had something big to do. Lives to change. People to help. Their own messages to spread." I think she's on to something. Avanti!

Carol Kirkpatrick

Retired International Opera Singer
Author of Aria Ready, The Business of Singing
Still maintains a Voice Studio in Denver, Colorado

Introduction

"It only takes a spark to get a fire glowing, and soon
all those around can warm up in its glowing…" –Kurt Kaiser

Those are the first words from a song that I sang in what I
remember as my very first performance. My mother and I sang
it as a duet in front of our church congregation when I was
about eight years old. Looking back through where my life has taken me,
remembering that the words are about fire and light is not lost on me,
and actually a little bit funny. Life has a way of giving us these little clues
about how we are supposed to use our gifts, and had I known then what
I know now I probably would have learned how to share them much
faster.

When I sat down to write this book, I had absolutely no idea what
I was doing, or why I was doing it in the first place, which is pretty
hilarious considering the subject matter. After all, I've always had a lot to
say, but I have never been a writer and I've never been the kind of woman
who freely said everything that was really on her mind. In fact, that's a
habit of mine that I have to stay on top of every day. At the beginning
of this process, all I knew was that there were a set of powerful words,
lessons, and stories inside of me that I needed to get out into the world.

Then one day, it occurred to me. In the theater, there is a concept called finding your light. It is something that I've had to practice when I'm on the other side of the camera getting photographs taken too. Essentially, it is the skill of knowing where the light is on the stage, and literally, physically moving your body into it so the audience can see your face. Many, many hours are spent getting the lighting right in the theater world. On the front end, the performers have special rehearsals just to move from spot to spot, finding the light so they learn to memorize where that warmth is and know exactly where to go to be seen. We also learn when other people will be standing in their own light so we understand that there is plenty to go around and everyone will be seen the way they are meant to once they get in their light.

On the back end, there is some masterful, brilliant person who has dreamt up an incredible lighting design meant to illuminate all the performers perfectly, and gone through a painstaking process of leading a crew in focusing each light just so, and uploading each and every lighting cue into the computer so every transition is flawless. It takes an extraordinary amount of teamwork to pull this off.

As a performer, I can also tell you that it takes quite a bit of courage to get used to this. There is this moment where, once you know your turn is coming up, you move your body forward and feel the warmth of the light hit your face. That's when you know in your bones that everyone can see you. Everyone can feel your energy and is waiting to hear the story you have to tell. And for you to fully bring it and give the audience an experience they will never forget, you have got to own that light. You must look like you were meant to be there, and take up all the space on stage that is required to deliver your point. It is scary and full of vulnerability, but it is a must because someone in that audience needs what you have to give them.

Many others in the arts, from painters to photographers, know this concept well too. If you are not positioning your subject in a way that allows the light to shine on it properly, the essence of what you are trying to communicate will not show itself to the audience correctly. Light is critical, and if there is something you are called to do, you have to allow yourself to step into it so you can be seen. If you are not positioning yourself in a way that allows the light to shine on you properly, you will never reveal the essence of what you hope to communicate to the audience. Taking this a step further, you also have to move some things around in your heart and soul to fully allow the essence of your gifts to exude from your presence when it's needed most. The light outside of you interacts with the light inside of you to help you share all your gifts with others.

This book will help you move through the steps that clear away many of the things that block you from your light. The mindset tricks fear plays on us, the distractions we put in our own way in the form of too-busy schedules and too-long To-Do lists, all of those things can keep you from letting your little light shine or even worse, feeling that you don't have one in the first place. Some days, it is excruciatingly hard to be at your best. But what I want for you is to have the tools available to shake off whatever is keeping you down so you can get yourself back into a space of lightness, and look at yourself with love at the end of the day knowing you were your favorite self anyway.

We all have something that lights us up inside, and when we share it with others, it lights them up too because they can feel our joy and our bliss and can't help taking a little bit of that energy for themselves. This creates the most unbelievable ripple effect. Now your light begins to spread like a book of matches lit on fire because you had the courage to tap into your greatest gifts with gusto and joy and do what you felt called to do. This allows you to give others the tools and strength they need to do the same. That spark ignites the spark in others, and before you know it, the world has changed in some way for the better because you stepped up. Because you shined brightly.

So, what's stopping you? Is it fear? Uncertainty? Overwhelm? Stress? Lack of support? Lack of clarity? What is blocking you? What is in your way? What is upstaging your light? What do you do on the days you feel stuck? Those days when you've gotten off track or you're not feeling inspired or motivated or you've fallen off the horse and don't know how to get back on track? These days happen to the best of us, so it isn't about perfection, it's about creating the habits that support your desire, and teaching yourself how to seek out that light and stand in it at all times in a way that is sustainable. Most of us have something that needs to be shifted in order to allow us to fully embrace the power of the thing we want to share with the world, but sometimes it's hard to even take those first steps from inspiration toward guided action until you handle it. And even then, the process of letting go of your need to control the outcome is something that must become a daily practice.

In your day-to-day life, there are many tools you can employ as you move through life to help make sure your light is shining at its brightest. Life is full of ups and downs, and in those moments where you feel it dim there are so many tools you can have at your disposal to reset, regroup, refresh, and step back into your light and into flow. You may have picked this book up because you wanted to kick some bad habits to the curb. And while, yes, we will certainly be doing a lot of that, I hope to give you so much more. The lessons I am going to teach you in the following pages have changed my life, and the lives of the many students and clients I've been honored to serve. You see, when you really change your habits, and I mean really get in there to do the dirty work required to change them for good, you can finally allow yourself to see how much you are worth. And when you finally fully believe in how much you are worth… let me tell you there is no turning back. That's when the magic happens, and it really gets good. If it did for me, I know it can for you too.

If you have a big mission that you are called to... The kind that won't leave you alone... That you are a little bit afraid of... There are some things you must have in place first to bring it into the light... To really be able to give of yourself in a way that changes the world no matter how big or how small... You must get it together. Here is what I mean. I teach my clients something called the L.I.G.H.T. Formula:

L - Leverage Your Mission

The importance of defining your core values, writing a powerful mission statement, and developing a vision statement for yourself. Then going beyond having something written down into learning how to use them in your daily life so they can give you the clarity to stay laser-focused on the things you want to accomplish.

I - Integrate Your Strengths

Understanding how you process information, what you naturally do best, and what your optimal environment is for getting things done. Once you know how you work best, you can access those superpowers anytime you need them.

G - Galvanize Your Efficiency

Learning how to create the systems and structures that help you get more of the right things done in less time. These sustainable productivity methods ensure that you consistently move towards your goals no matter what life throws at you, without sacrificing time with your loved ones.

H - Honor Your Recovery

Cultivating self-care routines that are truly revitalizing and adding strategies and mindset tools to help you bust through procrastination and overwhelm. We also explore how making a creative outlet part of your self-care routine increases your quality of life.

T - Transform Your Relationships

Creating and maintaining meaningful relationships in an increasingly digital world. These tools for leadership, listening, and communicating your story will help you develop the beautiful connections that are the lifeblood of everything we do.

In the following pages, I'll share stories about how these concepts have made an impact in my life and give you practical tools for how you can apply them to your own. I decided to put this all down into a book because I felt that someone, somewhere, needed to hear what I had to say because they had something big to do. Lives to change. People to help. Their own messages to spread. But for one reason or another, they were getting in their own way and couldn't quite figure out how to make it happen.

If you are reading this book today, thank you. I truly hope that it has the words you need to hear to inspire you to become your most favorite version of yourself for the people you love the most. When you close this book and put it down, I want you to be so inspired that you cannot help but pause, take a breath, then sit down and rethink what your values and desires are so you can realign them with your mission and vision. Then, I want you to take one step towards making that a reality by putting things in motion to fully embrace your unique essence. Just one small change will shift it all, and I want you to believe you can finally do it.

CHAPTER 1

In Case No One's Told You Lately, You're Worth It

"You're a shining star
No matter who you are
Shining bright to see
What you could truly be."
–Maurice White, Larry Dunn, and Philip Bailey

Y ou're worth it. Those three words have an incredible amount of power. It's kind of insane really, how many feelings three simple, short, little words can evoke. Fear. Joy. Sadness. Elation. Even physical reactions like tears. I'm not sure how this happens, but so many brilliant, beautiful women I know move through life feeling as if they are somehow not worth brilliant, beautiful things. Not worth joy, or freedom, or love, or whatever it is that is their heart's desire. But that's not true. You are worth it. You just need to believe it.

The first time someone told me I was worth it, it caught me completely and totally off guard. I was close to 30 years old, and after a particularly rough voice lesson my teacher and mentor, Carol, gave me a huge hug, then placed her hands on my shoulders, looked me deep in the eyes, and explained that while she knew it was tough and she was hard on me, if she let me get away with things she would be doing me a disservice because I was too talented. Then she hugged me close again and said softly in my ear, "You're worth it."

At first, I wasn't sure why she would say such a thing to me. Of course, I was worth it, right? Wasn't I? But it didn't take long for all of the thoughts and feelings to start flooding my mind and soul that I thought I had put to bed long ago.

Before I continue, let me paint you a picture of what I was like at this point in my life because you would not be able to recognize me. I had recently completed a graduate degree at a very prestigious university, and I was working full time as an administrative assistant for an incredible organization. It was a great job for a young singer. It paid well, had amazing benefits, gave me some time off here and there for auditions, and was full of wonderful people. I should have been very happy, but I couldn't enjoy the job because I had found myself in the crosshairs of the office bully.

I have been one of the very fortunate people who did not experience a lot of bullying growing up. In school, I had a lot of friends from many different cliques, and most people were very nice to me. So, to wind up in a situation where I was being picked on in an office as an adult was something that caught me pretty off guard. For over three years, I would go to work every day, wondering what I would accidentally do to make my co-worker mad. Would I respond to an email without enough information? Would I respond to an email with too much information? Would I say hello to her in the hallway when she didn't want to hear me speak? It was anybody's guess, but it was always something.

No matter how hard I tried to please this woman and just focus on doing my job well, she was never happy with me and made sure everyone knew it. Hearing her talk about me behind my back at a volume I was obviously meant to hear became a regular occurrence. It was so bad, in fact, that one by one every single one of my other colleagues pulled me aside and said something like, "Try not to let her get to you, she's just jealous that you're smart and talented and are doing great in the position she used to be in."

You would think that would have made me feel better, hearing from so many people that it was her and not me, and that I should just keep doing what I was doing, but that part did not stick. All I could focus on was that someone was treating me badly, and even though I thought I should stand up for myself, I just couldn't bring myself to do it. I was young, desperately wanted to do well at this job so I could keep it for as long as possible, and I hadn't quite learned the skill of standing up for myself yet. I was an insecure mousy little thing who let people walk all over me rather than be perceived as impolite or assertive.

Meanwhile, I was still plugging away at learning the ropes of the classical singing industry and trying to find my way around that. After a bit of success in the professional world of opera, my momentum began to stall. My singing seemed to be getting worse instead of better, and I noticed that where I once had the stamina to sing for hours at a time, I could only make it about 20 minutes before getting vocally fatigued.

It wasn't long before my performances started to dwindle down, and my audition opportunities began to disappear as well. After a trip to the ENT - those amazing ear, nose, and throat doctors who take incredible care of singers everywhere - I got the news that while my voice was mostly fine, my vocal technique was not. I needed to do some serious work on my breathing and some other important things if I wanted to regain my stamina and sing the way I used to. On top of that, I was diagnosed with acid reflux and a pretty serious allergy problem, which meant that my entire voice box was a tender inflamed mess most of the time.

This is not the kind of thing a grown-up singer with a brand new Master's degree wants to hear. There I was, spending forty hours of my week at a job where I was made to feel less than, while trying to understand why my instrument wasn't working and searching for a way to fix it. The whole situation made me feel pretty worthless, and like I had somehow messed up my own voice, the thing I cherished most. Maybe I hadn't been practicing correctly. Maybe I wasn't smart enough to recognize bad advice. Those are the kinds of thoughts that started to fill my head. Before long, I began to think that maybe I wasn't cut out for this career after all. I decided I probably didn't deserve it anyway, and spent many tearful nights wondering why I wasn't good enough.

That's when I met Carol. In our earliest lessons, she listened to my story and my dreams, and explained to me that everything I thought I knew about having a career as an opera singer was wrong. She told me that studying to be a professional singer has a way of forcing you to be vulnerable and puts you all the way out there. You spend a lot of time stripping away bad habits and rebuilding them with good ones, while hearing a lot of "No, do it again" in the process.

I think a lot of things are like that. When you have a gift or a calling that you want to share with the world, you work very hard to become great at it, in any industry. But that gap between where you are and where you want to be can seem so wide. And the work that it takes to cross it can really wear you down sometimes.

In the moment that Carol told me I was worth it, I realized very quickly that I was walking through life acting like I was worth it, but not really believing way deep down that I truly was. That is the crucial step. If you don't believe it fully, you'll have a much harder time wading through those hard days when you're caught up in the work. Carol knew this struggle well and could see in my eyes that I needed to hear that I was worth it. She knew that would crack something open that would help me get past my fears and insecurities so I could get on with it and share what

I had to give. This woman was able to see all of the gifts inside of me, and she knew that I couldn't quite get to them myself yet, so she helped me move closer towards them with those three words. For someone so powerful and sure of herself to wrap me up in her arms, squeeze me tight, and whisper those words into my ear... that shook something loose in a major way. Her saying that was like giving me permission to finally believe it and stop holding myself back. To stop acting like I wanted one thing, while secretly trying to convince myself that I wasn't really worth having all my dreams come true and that someone else should have what I wanted.

It was at that moment that I knew something had to change if I didn't want to keep moving through my life half committing to things. I would never be happy like this, not because I didn't have success, but because I would never give myself permission to truly play full-out in this game of life. To go big, and to have what I wanted. That's right, I said to have what I want. Not chase or go after or any of that, but to actually have it. Live it. Breathe it. Taste it. Walk and talk it. And, my dear reader, life is too short to not have what you want and feel happy and at peace. Because when you think about it, if you are not moving through life in a way that really fulfills you - whatever that looks like for you - then part of you is always going to feel like it's out of alignment. And then you will never really be able to give back all your wonderful gifts to the people who need it, and that is a terrible shame.

It's time for you to start moving through life with your best stuff, so you can give your best stuff. To do that, you must do the work to believe that you are, in fact, an amazing magnificent creature who is worthy of greatness and good things. Is it easy to get to that spot? Absolutely not, because the thought of minimizing ourselves in order to lift others up is so ingrained in us that we start to convince ourselves that others are somehow worth more than we are. It takes some serious transformational deep discovery work to undo that. Additionally, when reaching your heart's desires means stepping outside of the box and outgrowing the people and things you have always been comfortable around, it can be even harder. Growth of that magnitude requires you to be so tough and love yourself so much that you barely even notice what other people say about you. When you reach this point, you care less about the commentary because you know how much you're worth even if others don't. You know that you are priceless and have gifts and talents no one else does.

Is your worth tied to your job? How about your relationship status? What about how much money you have, or the car you drive, or the kind of home you live in? Because let me tell you, if you are attaching your self-worth to any of those external things, you will never gain full access to all of your amazingness. Any of those things could change at any moment. And then what? If you finally leave that job you hate but makes all your friends look up to you because you look amazing on paper, does that mean you are somehow worth less (notice I said worth less, not worthless) because now you're doing something different? No, it most certainly does not. But you are the one who needs to know that because somewhere out there is someone who'll give you some shade for it. And in those moments, you need to be able to stand up straight and tall and look them in the eye and… just not care. When you know in your bones that you made a decision to change your life and have what you want no matter how it makes you look, you will notice a little extra pep in your step and lightness in your heart. And that is something that you are totally 100% worth.

I have the complete and total privilege and honor of working with some absolutely incredible young musicians. One of the biggest hurdles we navigate together in their private voice lessons is getting them to believe that they are worthy of having careers in the music industry. It's very counter-intuitive, because so many people I talk to assume that these young musicians, or any musicians, actors, or people who long to spend their days in the spotlight, are star-struck little things who are in it for the attention and the accolades. That could not be further from the truth. In fact, they are some of the hardest working people I know, and frankly we all better watch out when they grow up because they are going to do some incredible things. But I digress. These teens want so badly to get on stage and use the art they've worked so hard to create as a vehicle to bare their souls, and hope that someone out there in the audience feels it as deeply as they do. But a conversation that comes up far too often is "I don't think I'm good enough to do this."

That is a terrible shame. First of all, good enough for who? For you. Your biggest critic. We all have a tiny voice inside of us somewhere that loves to bring all our insecurities and fears to light when we embark on a big goal. That's the person causing all this trouble and making you think you're not good enough. This doesn't just come up for my young singers, it comes up in some way, shape, or form for nearly every woman I know and a whole lot of the men too. Whatever the "it" is, from developing a more efficient way to clean your bathroom to crushing a sales goal at work so you can become employee of the month, every now and then that voice creeps in to remind you that whatever you're doing, it's not good enough. And why is that? Because it's not where you want it and there are things to improve? No… I would challenge you to flip that around and start to see if maybe what's really going on is you thinking that on some level buried deep down, you don't think you are really worthy of the thing you wish to have. Maybe you don't think you're worthy of having a fabulous home, or an amazing job, or a sassy new purse, or in the case of my students, the right to get on stage and tell a story through music regardless of the skill level they are currently at. By making it about the thing and not you, you can shine that light in the other direction and keep pretending it's okay to play small and deny yourself. But let me tell you that doesn't work. Eventually, you will wake up and be so mad that you've let so much time go by without owning your worth. If you are here reading this, you are probably there.

So, it's time to move past all that and figure out why. Why do we do this to ourselves? You are worthy of having the things you want. Not for any other reason other than you are uniquely you, and you are worth it.

To take this one step further, if you don't fully recognize and own your worth, you won't be able to get anyone else to either. We do this thing to ourselves where we run around being so upset that other people don't recognize our gifts and talents, when we don't even advocate for them ourselves! No one knows how brilliant you are more than you do. Once you own that, and begin to walk through your life without being so fearful that people will think negatively of you simply because you refuse to settle for less than you're worth, I cannot even describe to you how many things will begin to open up for you. It's as if you turn on this little light inside of you that shines on all the wonderful things you bring to this planet. And as it shines internally it grows and grows and spreads throughout your whole body and soul, so you begin to feel it in every cell. Suddenly, just like that, you are changed forever because you can recognize your own light. Once you get a taste of that, there is no going back. And then, the real magic happens. As you begin to let yourself light up with your own magnificence it becomes impossible to dim it, so you'll begin to see it grow brighter and light up the other people around you. That, my friends, is an incredible thing.

Now, I hear you saying, "How dare I just light up other people who don't want it?"

Well to that I say, who cares? Why should you dull your own light because someone somewhere feels like standing in the dark? The people who can't handle your worth will self-select themselves into stepping right on out of it. And thank goodness because you don't have time to be dealing with that anyway. You must have the mindset that you are already successful, believe that you can do it, and understand that you are WORTH IT, or you will never allow yourself to grow and change. You have too many fabulous things to do, and too much joy to go and experience to be bothered with all that. But here's the other thing. There is without a doubt somebody out there who desperately wants what you have to give. Someone already recognizes how beautiful and priceless it is because they need what you've got to change their own life. If you keep hiding and refusing to step it up, they will never find you and that is truly a tragedy. So, let's go get it together, shall we?

In the next chapter, we'll talk about what happens inside of you when you feel that part of you that is ready to feel worthy of good things shake itself loose, and the journey of change you're about to embark on. While it isn't an easy one, it is one of the most fulfilling roads you will ever travel, and the rewards will be greater than you thought possible. We'll talk about some things you can expect, and how you can prepare yourself to move through the feelings of discomfort that accompany major change. As you read on, I encourage you to have a journal with you to keep track of your thoughts, and any feelings and emotions that come up for you during this process. Take a moment to review the points of reflection at the end of each chapter. The clarity you'll gain from the questions will act as little points of light that guide you along the way and help keep you grounded during the transformation. Revisit them as often as you like and celebrate yourself for wherever you are starting from. Change is coming, but I assure you, you will be glad it did.

Points of Reflection:

- *Is there an area of your life where you feel like you aren't playing full-out?*
- *If yes, what do you think is holding you back from going for it?*
- *Do you find yourself placing your worth on external things, like cars, jobs, money in the bank, or other material things?*

- *What role does fear play in your life when it comes to reaching for what you want?*
- *What would it take for you to know that you are worthy of all the amazing things you desire in life?*
- *Are there any places in your life where you struggle to set boundaries or let people walk all over you?*

CHAPTER 2

Get Comfortable with the Discomfort

*C*hange is hard. So hard that it's one of the things that strikes enough fear in people's hearts to cause fights, ruin relationships, and keep people in terrible situations for decades. What is it about changing something we are familiar with that is so scary for us? Furthermore, why does the idea of branching out from what's comfortable fill us with so much dread and trepidation, even when we know it's for our own good and will work out better? Over the next few pages, we're going to dive into the concept of change, and why we are so resistant to it even when it is a positive thing. We'll discuss how you can learn to view change with excitement instead of stress and anxiety, and embrace those moments of uncertainty with love and appreciation instead of fear.

"And the day came when the risk to remain tight in a bud was more painful than the risk it took to blossom." –Anaïs Nin

The first time I heard this quote I was staring right into the eyes of the opportunity to make a massive change. It was after I had finished graduate school, and I had been working with Carol for a while. Despite enjoying living in St. Louis, I knew that something had to change if

I wanted to make some strides towards my professional goals. I didn't know what needed to change, only that I was growing increasingly restless. Agitated and irritated at nothing in particular. It wasn't that I was unhappy, per se, but more like I just could not get comfortable. Doing the same old routine every day left me feeling like something was missing, and physically I constantly needed to stretch or shift or move a part of my body. It was a very odd sensation that I really felt in different ways. I recognized it as something that I'd felt before, but I couldn't identify what was going on.

Then I saw that quote. I instantly realized that I was in a position I'd been in before: my current life circumstances no longer supported my desires and if I wanted to fix that something needed to change. Of course, I instantly felt fear and doubt wash over me, because what comes with change? Growth and uncertainty, and right on the tails of those two come discomfort. I was so comfortable with my situation that it was making me physically uncomfortable, but to get out of it I would have to make myself even more uncomfortable for a little while. Quite a catch 22, isn't it?

It's a bit like the feeling you get when you're sitting in the same position for a while and your foot goes to sleep. Some signals go off in your brain that tell you your foot isn't getting enough blood flow and it's time to move it. So, you start to get uncomfortable and eventually move a little bit and change positions. But then it hits. That awful pins and needles feeling as the blood flow returns to your foot, and you start to wonder if it was better to just leave it asleep to begin with. You know logically that it's not that bad and it won't last long, but really you just want it to be done so you can take a breath and put weight on your foot again. Finally, your foot stops tingling and goes back to normal and all is well.

This is similar to what those big life changes feel like. We know something isn't right, we resist for a little while until we don't have a choice, then we experience some discomfort - sometimes a massive amount of discomfort, let's be honest here - and then the dust settles, and we're fine. Despite all the challenges and hard stuff we just went through, and all the scariness associated with leaping into something without totally knowing how it's going to pan out, we're okay. Perhaps a little banged up, but generally okay. And if the change has left you not so okay, there are resources to help with that too so you can get whatever support you need to find your way back to okay.

But that's really the root of it, isn't it? All that fear that's keeping us in the discomfort of our situation is because we're afraid that we'll make a choice that will leave us with more of it. The reality is that change comes with a little bit of risk, and there is the possibility that when we leap into the unknown it will take longer than we'd like to be comfortable again. Flowers have no idea what is going to happen to them when they open up. But they do it anyway because they have outgrown the bud. So, the question I'd like you to ponder is what will you do to help yourself get comfortable with the idea of discomfort? It could be anything from the desire to reach a goal, the motivation to do something for yourself or your loved ones, or even to break free from something you no longer want in your life. This is for you to discover and decide.

This process of growing and transforming into the person you are meant to be is not an easy one. It is going to require you to step up in a big way, stop making excuses for yourself, own up to what you really want, take the steps to get it, and let go of the habits and people holding you back. Yes, sometimes the people who love you the most are the same people holding you in place right where you are. This takes some serious courage. It is not easy, or everyone would be diving into personal development and running around having exactly what they want. But if you look around, you will see how many people are stuck right where they are because they cannot bring themselves to break through the barriers and do the work to change. I would love for you not to be one of those people.

You'll know when it's time. You'll know because things will just feel… off. It's almost like there are invisible walls pressing up against you (that's that bud you're too big for, my friends). It's not hurting you… it's just not right. If you're anything like me you'll start to be more and more dissatisfied with things that never bothered you before because while they may have served an important purpose on your life's journey at one point, you don't need those same things anymore. It's time for something else now and deep down, your intuition knows that you won't be happy until you go for it. At this point, the only way to get you to change something is to make you feel slightly uncomfortable with what used to be comfortable. No one ever grows or changes or does anything if we aren't uncomfortable in the first place.

I've been going through all these changes in my business lately, like working with bigger teams, more high profile clients, and dealing with numbers with a whole bunch of zeros. Is this right in line with what I want to be doing? Absolutely. But every day I have to challenge myself to grow a little more, shine a little brighter, and actually walk the walk of the person I know I can be who is fully capable of handling big executive duties and the pressures that come with them. If you really want to be good at what you are doing, you have to be willing to go through that painful process of growing into a new version of yourself over and over again. I admit, it's challenging for me too. It requires me to stretch a lot, but even if it's a little uncomfortable and a lot scary sometimes, it's always AWESOME on the other side because I'm fully being who I was meant to be instead of hiding, playing small, or playing someone else's game entirely.

In addition to managing your own emotions when you embark on the journey of facilitating this kind of growth, what else should you be prepared for? There is something interesting that happens to the people we love as we start to go through rapid transformational changes. Have you heard the story about what happens to crabs when they wind up in a barrel? It's a pretty popular reference in the entrepreneurial circle, and I've heard many teachers mention it. Essentially, crabs do this thing where if one of them tries to climb out the barrel the others will grab it and try to pull it back in. That sounds a little ridiculous, considering that the bucket is going to take all those crabs to someone's dinner table, but when you think about it, they aren't really so different than we are as humans. What happens when you make a decision that is different from the way your family has always done something? All of a sudden, every aunt, cousin, and all the pets have something to say about why it will or won't work so you forget that you even brought it up and go on about your day.

Maybe you decide to go forward with it, but maybe you also decide that it's not worth it and let it go. This is where you need to recognize that other people's noise is going to be a big part of the journey. When you change, other people - many times out of love for you and the hope that they'll be protecting you if something goes wrong, but sometimes out of fear that you are going to go and get yourself happy by being different and that doesn't make them look or feel so good - will start ragging on your idea. If you go through with it, strangers will start ragging on it just to throw their two cents in. You will find that as you change, suddenly a whole lot of people have a whole lot to say, and sometimes it's not awesome.

If you've ever woken up with some kind of amazing idea, or decided on a whim to break out of your usual style choice and wear a color that you typically don't, I'm sure you can see the faces of the people who are so shocked at you breaking out of your routine and wanting to try something new. You must get comfortable with criticism and learn to make friends with it. Not only that but get comfortable with deciphering which criticism is useful, and which criticism will hold you back more than it will help. In the case of the latter, a great skill to develop is learning to say to yourself: This criticism isn't helpful to me and I don't even need to let it get to me. When you can stop taking everything so personally, you take the power back over the criticism-disguised-as-advice you will inevitably receive. Then, you can easily see what to take seriously and what to ignore.

There is a woman in my life whom I have known for several decades now. She is wonderful and I love her dearly, and while we get along very well, she has always been really confused by what I do for a living. And I'm not talking, doesn't quite understand the high-level ins and outs of the classical music or consulting industries, or the critical metrics one tracks as an entrepreneur. I mean after all this time, she cannot grasp the very basic, simple, foundational elements of what I do or why I do it. Of course, I know that to people who chose a traditional path my life is very confusing and doesn't make a lot of sense, so I try to be as patient and understanding as possible when I explain things to the new relationships in my life. But even now, twenty years into our relationship, this woman still asks the same questions every time we talk about it. It got to the point where I started to wonder if she was actually listening to me, or just wilfully trying to misunderstand. Did she want to talk to me and just made up a reason because she couldn't think of anything else? Was she hoping I would give her a different answer? Was I being terribly unclear in my explanations? There are only so many ways I can explain how I book a concert without starting to wonder if I'm crazy.

Eventually, I began tuning it out and would just kind of go through the motions of the conversation until she got tired of hearing the same unsatisfactory response and changed the subject to what was going on with her. However, in the early years of my consulting business when it started to really take shape and grow, I finally began to pinpoint what the actual problem was.

I will never forget the day when this finally clicked for me, and it changed my whole outlook on relationships with loved ones. There had been a new development in my business, and I reminded myself aloud that I needed to check in with my assistant about a certain metric. I happened to be within earshot of this woman when I said it. Naturally, her first question was, "You have an assistant?"

I said yes and explained a little bit more about what she did for me. That led to a brief explanation about sales funnels and digital marketing when she paused for a moment and said, "So, things are going well then? Well okay."

I started by diving into my typical response when someone unfamiliar with what I do asks about how my business is going, but I want to spare them from my obsessive excited babbling about funnels and conversion rates and whether or not my marketing strategy worked in quarter two. I learned pretty quickly how fast that makes someone's eyes glaze over and decided to cut my losses. These are the responses I give: "Yes, it's been an exciting and challenging year and I've learned a great deal," or "I've achieved some fantastic goals and I'm really looking forward to what's coming up next."

They are just vague enough to satisfy the person asking without inspiring them to ask more questions. But this time, I nearly stopped mid-sentence because for the first time ever I finally recognized the look on her face. There she sat, while I was talking about how nicely things were moving along, and stared back at me with a look of disappointment. It was unmistakable. There was a legit frown on her face, and she was shaking her head as she responded. She was actually bummed out that I was doing well and moving forward in my business, the way I had always wanted.

I could hardly believe it. What I had always mistaken for confusion and misunderstanding was actually something else entirely. I finally understood why I left every conversation with her so frustrated and hurt: she would say she was supporting me but her expression and body language, plus complete lack of understanding said otherwise, and I was always totally confused by it.

That day, everything finally made sense to me and I saw it clearly. As much as she loved me, and was supportive on the surface, it was still painful for her to see things going well. To her, that meant that I was getting further and further from living the life she had envisioned I would. Here I was off doing something completely out of her comfort zone, making choices that I'm sure seemed like a risk - and sometimes were - while stepping further away from what everyone else in our circle was doing. In other words, I had left the bucket.

In her mind, I was doing the exact opposite of what she thought I should be doing, which involved me living close by, getting a stable, traditional job, and starting a family around the same age she did instead of several years later. Naturally, this caused her to feel concern, disappointment, and probably some sadness too. I was different. My choices were different. Our relationship had become different because of it. I was never coming back to the bucket. I'm not sure whether she was more disappointed that I chose to leave, or that she chose to stay. Either way, I was making it more obvious to her. In that moment when I finally saw the truth, it was like a weight was lifted off of me.

I could love her dearly, but I needed to stop hoping she would understand what I did and quit trying to win her approval. Even if I checked all the typical life marker boxes - make good money, get married, buy a house, start having babies, etc. she would never fully support me because I didn't do it her way. The only way to make her proud would be to give it all up, throw in the towel, and get back in the proverbial bucket by doing the exact same thing she and so many others did, and apologize for daring to do my own thing to begin with. And since that wasn't happening for me anytime soon, I had to let go of my attachment to her feelings.

That was the last time we spoke about my business or any other major life choices I did or didn't make. All of our conversations since then have been pretty light-hearted and focused on her, and if she brings up one of those same questions she's always asked, I give her a short answer and change the subject. This is a much better arrangement. We still get along great, but I don't leave every conversation feeling totally defeated. Instead, I share my business wins and losses with the people in my inner circle who truly get me and want nothing more than to see me succeed on my own terms.

There will be many people like this in your life. Even if your "bucket" isn't jumping into entrepreneurship, once you decide to do something your own way and march to a different drum, someone will worry. You are going to cause someone some stress because you are highlighting the choices they didn't make but always wanted to. Once it starts working for you, there will be a bit of "who does she think she is" when you bounce by with all that pep in your step. But you cannot let it get to you. You have to let go of the desire to make anyone other than yourself proud, or the need to win anyone's approval or support. If you don't, you will constantly be trying to live up to someone else's impossible standard instead of the only important one: your own.

My mentor Carol always said, "What you think of me is none of my business," which is the title of one of her favorite books by Terry Cole-Whittaker, and that is one of the most freeing statements you can ever internalize.

She's right! What other people think of you isn't any of your business at all. Their opinion of you and what you're doing is a reflection of them, not you. You are the one who determines how well you sleep at night, and you should live each and every day making choices and taking actions that make you proud. You have to create a legacy that no matter how big or small, leaves you with a sense of pride and joy.

So, what do you do instead of succumbing to the need to make a bunch of other people proud by doing what they think you should do? For starters, you can decide what makes YOU proud of you. What are the things that determine how good you feel? Are those things in alignment with what you want? When you make this about you and hold yourself up to your standard of excellence and no one else's, suddenly this process and all the ups and downs that come with it become much easier.

You should also begin to insulate yourself with the people who will be proud of you no matter what, and truly get what you're about. Feel free to love those other people dearly and continue to keep up the relationships that matter to you, but don't let them drag you back down to their level of fear. Keep moving, and find the key people who will step up to push you forward, run alongside you, and even drag you with them for a little while on those days when things aren't going so well. Having support on this journey is critical, but it has to be the right kind. Once you find your new fancy shell or rock or whatever it is, you can wave to your friends in the bucket. You can even go visit and lean right over the side of it so they know you still care about them and remember where you come from. But don't you dare even think about getting back in.

Moving forward we'll begin to discuss what types of internal habits and mindset shifts you'll need to make to get the greatest momentum as you move along this path. It all starts with getting extremely clear on your mission, vision, and values, as those are the things that help you decide what you want most in life. Together, we'll explore how to get down to the core of uncovering what that is, and how you can apply it to your goals and more.

Points of Reflection:

- *How can you tell when it's time for you to change something? Looking back, what types of feelings came up in the days, weeks, or months before you made a big change?*

- *What sort of fears come up for you when you think about the concept of change?*
- *What excites you about the possibility of change?*
- *What makes you feel proud of yourself at the end of each day?*
- *Who are some people in your life that are always there for you, and will help you achieve your goals without question?*

CHAPTER 3

The Power of Knowing What You Want

*H*ave you ever woken up one day and wondered, how did I even get here and why am I even doing this? Then paused for a second only to realize that to your horror you don't even like the thing you're putting all this time, energy, and maybe money into? Yep. I've been there too. It sucks, and it's exhausting, draining, and not at all fun to go through that emotional rollercoaster. I mean, it brings up all kinds of questions about your judgment and your life choices that can really make you doubt yourself and the life you've built. Let's talk about what you can do to set yourself up for success here, and make sure that you really know what you want, how to course-correct if you find yourself going after something that doesn't fit that mold any longer, and perhaps most importantly, what to do if you feel like what you're working on is suddenly out of alignment with your values.

When I work with my clients, we do some deep exploration around uncovering what they really want out of life, and how to align that with their core values. We don't just leave it at the beginning or end of our process either, this is something that gets revisited regularly to make sure they are consciously setting goals that match up with their mission and vision. When you get into the habit of really tuning into those important things more and more frequently, it becomes easier to make decisions that pull you toward what really lights you up inside. At that moment, you learn how to not just know your personal mission in life, but you learn how to truly leverage it.

Understanding what you want is such a powerful thing, because once you know, you can make your plans and decisions around that, and get rid of all the extra noise that isn't serving you anymore. And when I say, what you want, I mean something that's so much bigger and greater than things like "I want more money" or "I want a bigger house" or whatever the thing is that you think is going to finally make you happy. I mean, what is it that you really want? What is that material thing going to get you towards?

Part of that is unpacking why you are here, what your purpose is, and how you can align your gifts with that. Because that is really where the spark can ignite some amazing things that ripple out from you for generations: matching up what you love, what you're good at, and what you really truly want. I realize this is a process and much easier said than done. So many times we walk around denying ourselves the opportunity to even acknowledge that we want something, that admitting to what that even is can be an impossible task. But I promise you, if you stop here for a moment and start asking what you want out of this life, you will begin to unlock some things inside of you that you didn't know were locked up. That is how this transformation begins. That is what makes going through this process of change and growth bearable because finally, you are giving it all you've got to have the life you want instead of the life somebody else said you should have.

Everything should start with your mission. At the beginning of our work together, Carol taught me how to create a mission statement for myself, the same way I did for my company. It has kept me on track in an amazing way, and I hope it does the same for you. When you can really zero in on your why, and how it relates to all the decisions that you make, it becomes very easy to maintain your momentum. Staying in tune with your why helps keep you motivated when things get hard and gives you the ability to say yes to the right things and no to the wrong things.

But how do you begin to uncover something as big and as meaningful as what your mission in life is? Fortunately, it is much simpler than we think it is, and the answer is already inside of us. You will find the seeds that grow into your mission and vision within the core values that you have carried with you all your life.

Your core values are the things that are so deeply ingrained within us that whether they are highlighted or violated, you can feel it in your bones. For example, if you see someone getting picked on and it makes you angry, chances are you have hit upon a core value. If you get incredible bliss from volunteering for your favorite organization, that's right - somewhere in there is a core value. When you feel an emotion that is accompanied by a visceral response in your body, that emotion is more than just a feeling. It is a signal that one of your values is greeting you.

To find them, start by listing a few memories from your life that really stick out, and what you learned from that experience. They can be positive events, negative events, or even influential people you've met along the way, as long as you remember it clearly. Here's an example: I remember everything about the moment I knew I had to be a performer. I was on stage in a musical in the tenth grade, and I remember the view of the crowd, the way my itchy costume felt, the hot lights, the smell of the theater, everything. When I recall this memory, I can instantly feel the excitement of the moment as if I were right back there. This taught me that performing music was more than just important to me – it would be a major part of my life.

Once you come up with three or four memories and list what you've learned, give each lesson a powerful word or short phrase that signifies its meaning. Using my example above, I could use words like creativity, music, imagination, etc.

Next, add a verb to each word or phrase to explain how you are going to carry your mission out. For example, things like inspire creativity, share beautiful music, or help others explore their imagination are all actionable phrases that really show off my core values. This is the basis of your mission statement. Once you have that in place, it's time to make a full statement out of the phrases. Be sure to include the following elements: What you are going to do, how you are going to do it, and who you are going to do it for - your friends, your family, your clients, your community, the planet, etc. Make it as big as you dare to dream! Use it often to help guide you. Keep it written somewhere but also commit it to memory so you can say it whenever you need to be reminded why you're doing what you're doing.

Once you have your values and mission in place, it's time to turn your attention to your vision. Think of it like this: if your mission is your why, your vision is your what. To get there, you must go a little deeper than deciding what it is that you want to create. Ask yourself questions like this: who do you want to impact? Why is it meaningful to them? What kind of outcome will this have on those who receive the benefits from it? What do you wish to see this becoming? And why does any of that matter? Here, you get the chance to look towards the future and envision how your light will shine in a bigger context. You will always be working towards your vision, and adding to it or reshaping it as necessary. Your mission keeps you moving in the right direction.

When these things are in place and you practice using them as tools, suddenly figuring out what you want becomes easy. It doesn't even have to be something that grand to work. Sometimes if I'm out buying a new outfit and can't make a decision, I'll hold both items up in the mirror and see which one is aligned with my mission and fits into my vision. Takes care of things right away. And of course, when it is a big decision, the more I lean into my mission when I plan and execute, the more ease I feel as I bring the creation to fruition. If you're feeling unsure about a decision, simply say your mission to yourself while thinking about the outcome you are taking action towards, and notice which feels right. You'll know.

The other side of this is learning how to recognize what you don't want, and looking at how your decisions, choices, and actions might be supporting that instead. That goes back to being able to unpack that moment where you woke up and asked, how did I get here, and being able to identify how you got there. What did you say yes to when you should have said no? What did you say no to when you should have said yes? How many times have you known deep down that you really truly didn't want to do, say, be, or have something but gone right ahead and did it anyway?

First and foremost, take a breath. Stop. Give yourself some grace here and recognize that it's not the end of the world. You're gonna be just fine and all is not lost. No matter how far away from your original desire you seem to have drifted, you can figure out a way to get back, or even start over entirely. Then, when you've had your moment, figure out what isn't working. Ask yourself, what don't you love? Why don't you love it? What is out of alignment with your goals and desires here? Be honest with yourself, and at this point in the process I don't even want you to stress over it. Getting too deep into trying to figure out how things ended up this way is for another day. I only want you to recognize what's not feeling right so you can figure out how to turn this into something that does.

Once you identify what you want to change, then we move on to the next part. The magical stuff. The truly amazing life-changing stuff. Right here, in this moment, you get to ask yourself what it is that you really want, and give yourself permission to get it. I know this seems simple, but how many days have you woken up thinking about all the things you *have* to do instead of the things you *want* to do? Even when you have responsibilities to handle and work to do, when you can line up your day-to-day with your heart's desire, and build your life around that you will see how quickly your have to's become want to's, and then even better still become get to's. That's when you can live your life as your best, and even the tedious boring parts of the process becomes a joy because you know they are contributing to the greater beauty of a life created on your terms and with all the things YOU want it to have in it.

I have recently been waking up earlier than normal saying, "I'm glad I get to wake up early today!" This is no small feat, and any of my close friends reading are surely laughing because they know that I am typically a night owl through and through. But here's the thing. Even though I'm much more comfortable staying up until all hours of the night, I've learned that I do my best when I get up a little earlier and ease into the day with a structured morning routine. When I'm at my best I do better work, and when I do better work, I get to see a little more of my vision come into focus each day. So, while I may not love the actual act of getting up early, I sure love the result that it gets me.

On the flip side, what do you do when you have a hard time figuring out what you want? Here's a silly example, that illustrates this concept well. Deciding on where to go for a bite to eat is one of those topics that can quickly cause drama between even the happiest pair of hungry people. I am one of those cliché women who never knows what she wants but simultaneously knows what she doesn't want; therefore, actually knowing exactly what I want. And if I settle for something I don't want instead of eating what I really wanted, I'll enjoy it but I won't be totally happy about it. My non-particular husband has put up with this for years. By now, he knows that simply asking me what I want to eat will result in a conversation that goes around and around for quite some time, and eventually we'll just end up getting something from the place right up the street because we tired ourselves out.

So, in recent years, he's changed his approach to see if he could crack my code. Occasionally he'll just say where we're going, not giving me a choice, which only works about half the time. Sometimes, he'll get an idea of where he wants to go and tell me what he feels like eating, which works most of the time. The method that has proven to be the most effective, however, is to just figure out what I don't want. He'll ask me where I want to go for dinner, and if I don't give him an immediate enthusiastic answer, but an "Ummmmm, I don't know yet" instead, he'll respond with questions about food. The conversation goes something like this:

> "What do you feel like for dinner?"
> "Oh, I don't know, whatever."
> "… Pizza?"
> "No."
> "A burger?"
> "No."
> "Chinese?"
> "No."
> "Okay, what sounds bad about those?"
> "Nothing in particular, I just maybe want something lighter."
> "Like a salad?"
> "NO."
> "Some soup?"
> "No… more like little bits of things."
> "Like a vegetable tray?"

This is when he starts to get a little warmer…

> "Sort of, but more than that."
> 'Does bread sound good?"
> "Ooooh yes."

"What about bread and cheese?"

"Yes!"

"So you want to go to the grocery store and get some bread, veggies, cheeses, etc. and have that for dinner?"

"Yes. Yes, that is exactly what I want. How did you know?"

I'm telling you he's a pro at this. It's become a game that he loves to win. Now, I'm not always this bad and it isn't always this tedious, but on those days when my brain has had enough creative thinking and processing and I just can't get to what I want, it really helps to start ruling things out like this so I can come out on the other side understanding what I truly do want.

You can apply this to your life too. If you are still searching for what truly makes your heart sing, that passion or purpose that lights your soul on fire and makes you want to shout it from the rooftops, that's okay. This is a process that takes patience and sometimes a bit of trial and error, along with the support of a trusted loved one. But the point is, sometimes when you're on your journey to self-discovery you might find that going through a period of working hard for something you DIDN'T want showed you what you really DO want, and you would have never known that otherwise. It is worth it in the end, and the tools you'll learn along the way make the journey that much more interesting!

It is inevitable that at some point or another we'll end up in a situation that we truly don't want to be in, and start to beat ourselves up while trying to figure out how to deal with it. How do you get yourself out of that spiral? And if you find that something must give, and something must absolutely change because you cannot live another second the way you are living, where do you even begin? Before we go any further, I want to make sure you know that you're not alone. So many of us have been in that same moment. Again, this is another great time to take a breath and gather your thoughts. No matter how big or how small this thing is that has to change, it's okay, and it's going to be okay, no matter what you decide. Even if there is some work ahead, you're going to be fine. Remember what we talked about earlier? You're still worth it. You can still have the life you want on your terms. You can still design your life around your heart's desires.

When it comes to course-correcting, let's spend a few minutes on the topic of what to do when you realize something just really isn't for you at all anymore and has got to go. Once you know something's gotta give, there is no turning back. Bringing that thought into your awareness somehow sets a chain reaction into motion that you will not be able to deny, and the momentum is going to happen with or without you. It's okay to be afraid. But it is not okay to let that fear keep you stuck right where you are.

So how exactly do you manage moving through these types of transitions? This is the part in the process where you must hang on tight to the idea of what you want because that is what is going to make all this discomfort worth it. So, go back to the first step of identifying your core values and your mission and vision. If you feel like they have changed, that is okay too. I've rewritten my own mission statement about four times now. When you feel like those are back where you want them, then you can look at the situation objectively and ask what isn't serving you anymore. If it's time to quit that job or leave that relationship, that's okay. If that project is doing nothing more than making you mad, give it to someone else and let go. But here is where you need to identify why that is so you can see any old habits popping up down the road that try to pull you off your path again. Knowing that at the end of the process, you'll be an even more incredible version of yourself who has achieved what you set out to will help drive you towards the end. After everything is said and done, you'll be tougher because you survived the scariness of a big change.

To add to this, consider that in many cases you have to grow into the person that is ready for the things you want. The thing itself is not going to change, so you have to step into the person that can receive it. At those times when you want to quit, or wonder if you made the wrong choice, or discover that you did, in fact, make the wrong choice and have to pivot into a totally different direction to get back on course, that mission and vision you have will be like a lighthouse. They will be there, shining in the distance, helping guide you back toward alignment, and letting you know that all will be well.

Coming up in the next chapter, we'll talk about all the amazing things that make you who you are, and how you can tap into them to enhance your mission and bring your vision to life faster than you ever thought possible.

Let's Recap:

Step 1   Let your emotions guide you to what your core values are.

Step 2   Give each of those values a word, and string those words together in a mission statement that sets your soul on fire.

Step 3   Dream up what the vision for your life is and let your mission lead the way.

Points of Reflection:

- *How often do you tune in with what you want on a deep level?*
- *Is there anything in your life that isn't serving your mission anymore?*
- *How can you tell that you are being pulled away from what you truly want?*
- *What can you do to get back to listening to your desires?*

CHAPTER 4

Your Uniqueness is On Your Side

ccept yourself as you are. This is a tough one, isn't it? The whole concept of accepting the things we don't love so much about ourselves is a difficult one to get on board with. This can be particularly challenging for those of us wired to obsess over personal development. I'm like this, and find that I'm on a quest to constantly improve myself, or work towards mastering something. That's great to a point, but if we can't love ourselves just as we are at this moment, and appreciate all that we've done so far on this journey, it can actually hold us back from moving forward. This is also a hard thing to do if you're the type who feels like you don't fit in anywhere, you're always going against the grain, or you haven't quite found your people yet. Let's take a look at how you can find a way to turn your perceived weaknesses into hidden superpowers.

One of the things that makes me angry is when I hear about someone telling people I care about that they aren't good enough because of xyz. That xyz is always something that is inherently unique to them, and not necessarily a bad thing. This happens a lot with my young students. Once in a while, a student will come to their lesson looking a little lower energy than usual. I always start each lesson asking how they are, because if something is going on in their lives it can be helpful to get it out of the way a little bit so we can have a more productive singing lesson. After all, when we get upset about something, we usually feel a physical lump in our throat and/or a pit in our stomach, and those are both areas that are critical to singing. It helps to keep them clear and working properly.

Every so often a student will arrive clearly upset about something. There is one occasion like this that is particularly stuck in my memory. One day, I asked this brilliant, hard-working, talented young woman how her day was, and she responded "Fine." Since this is not an unusual response for a teenager to give an adult, I almost let it go, but something told me to keep prying a little deeper. I asked a few more leading questions, and eventually got to the issue. She had a really rough day at school, and there had been an incident with her choir teacher. I wasn't sure where this was headed exactly, but as someone who has had more than her share of days where she didn't fit in with a choir, I could feel exactly what kind of emotional day she had gone through. She went on to tell me that she had gotten yelled at in class for being a bit chatty. That's a bummer, no one likes to get yelled at by a teacher whether it was something you were responsible for or not.

However, that wasn't the whole story. It's what happened afterward that made me want to reach through the computer screen of this online lesson to give her a hug and wipe her tears, then go make a phone call to the teacher. I wanted nothing more than to explain why his behavior was thoughtless and inappropriate, and that it may take years to undo one comment bestowed upon a fragile teen girl. However, I calmed myself down and kept listening to her. After she got in trouble for talking, she was a little upset and showed it visibly as they moved into the rest of the rehearsal. The director took notice of this and called her out in front of the class for being too sensitive. Of course, that did nothing but make her more upset, and he went on to say you will never be successful if you are always this sensitive.

I was shocked. I could not understand how a teacher could say that to a student. I tried to give him the benefit of the doubt for a second because I know that sometimes students mishear or misinterpret something you say and don't quite understand the concept. But this was different. These were his exact words to her. And really, even if they weren't, if the words were slightly different, they were still close enough that that's what she heard, and worse, that's what she believed.

So there she sat, on the other end of the screen looking like her entire future was crumbling before her eyes and there was nothing to be done about it, while I sat on the other side trying to find the words to help her see that that teacher was oh so wrong in his assessment. All I wanted her to know in that moment was that she was not too sensitive. She was wonderful. She had this incredible gift of feeling her feelings so deeply and so fully that sometimes they just poured out of her whether she wanted them to or not. Not only that, but she could see things in other people and in the world and be so moved by them that those feelings gave her a well of inspiration that chose to manifest itself as a talent for writing music. That's how she expressed herself the best.

I don't remember what I told her. But it was something along the lines of this: Your sensitivity, this thing that you feel is a weakness so big that it would threaten your ability to be successful, is actually more like a secret superpower. It is what will help you change the world. It's what will allow you to heal other people. Forget all that about fitting in or achieving your goals or whatever… This beautiful sensitivity of yours is a gift that you just haven't learned how to use yet. But you will, and when you do, everyone better look out because the light you have in you will shine so bright it will be blinding.

My student has something in common with all of us. We all have something that we feel is some kind of major flaw that's keeping us from being, doing, or having what we want. Keeping us from fitting in, or being heard, or making us feel like we are perpetually misunderstood but please hear me when I say, what if it isn't? What if it doesn't have to be this way? What if we took that thing that we so desperately wanted to change about ourselves and picked it up, cradled it in our arms, loved on it for a moment, and thanked it? What if we thanked our uniqueness? Our weirdness. The thing that makes us stick out. What if we finally learned how to use it as a tool that helped us step fully into our light so we could do the work we are put on this planet to do?

How would your life change if you could do that? Who else's life could you change if you operated from that space instead of a space where you woke up every day wishing away that secret gift before you even learned what to do with it? What could you get done? How would you move through your day? Would you be afraid and ashamed, or would you dance with joyful gratitude because you knew that your special thing was here in your bones for a reason and you couldn't wait to jump out of bed and use it?

Let's talk about how you can begin to figure this out. Many people are familiar with the concept of Extraversion vs. Introversion. Everyone's a little bit of both, but for most of us, we tend to lean one way or the other. When I was a little girl, I used to get in trouble for speaking loudly, which resulted in me spending many years as an adult speaking very softly. It wasn't until I was well into my thirties that I realized people found me difficult to hear because I was afraid of being perceived as too loud. I did some internal work around why I was so worried about that, and came to discover that among other things, I had some baggage around feeling unheard. So, if I used my voice to speak loudly and still couldn't get my point across then what was the point? It took many years to release those beliefs about myself, and reteach myself how to speak at an audible volume.

Talking loudly is one of the stereotypes that extraverts are known for. While it's true that anyone can talk loudly if they choose to, it was so helpful for me to know that what I was already wired for, gaining energy from lots of social interaction, was right in line with another trait of people like me - talking loudly. It may seem simple, but it really helped me to know that this was a part of who I was and I could use it freely, or tone it down if I chose to.

Now, what about introverts? We live in a society that is heavily geared towards extraversion, and places a lot of value on being outgoing, attending social functions, etc. For the introverts among us who need some solitude to recharge their batteries, this can get draining quickly. A few years ago, one of my introverted friends expressed to me that she wished more people understood how they felt, and that the world didn't seem to value quiet and self-reflection the same way they did. This left them feeling as though people thought something was wrong with them. I responded by telling her how some of the deepest connections and most incredible conversations I have are with introverts because we dive right into deep and meaningful exchanges. So, for those of you introverts who aren't sure if you should ask a powerful question to an extravert when you are ready, you absolutely should. It's something that makes you incredible and shouldn't be shied away from.

If you had told me 10 years ago that I would have two businesses - one as a professional singer, and another as an in-demand high performance consultant - I probably would have laughed. I mean, the singing makes sense, but the consulting part? No way. Not for this starving artist. I was born to sing on stage, and that is it. Unfortunately (maybe fortunately?) sometimes the universe really does know what's best and insists that we step into the roles we were meant to fill whether we like it or not. So here I sit, writing this book that seems to be begging to be written, and getting ready to teach some brilliant people how to achieve the levels of focus an opera singer has so they can be their best for the ones they love.

I haven't always been obsessed with personal development… In fact, I used to kind of laugh and scoff at the idea of all these self-help books claiming to help you live your best life. That was until I realized that I was further from living my best life than I ever dreamed I would be because I was so caught up in being mad about all the parts of me I thought were weaknesses that needed to be hidden. Once upon a time I was downright unhappy. Don't get me wrong, there are still plenty of days where things aren't all sunshine and rainbows for me, but overall, I can bounce back from them much quicker. And now, when challenges do come up, I can move through them with excitement and a sense of joy, instead of the crushing fear and disappointment that I used to feel. And that, to me, is worth all of the craziness that has been this ride of the last ten years.

Here's where my story began. I grew up in a very musical family. My mother sang – still sings - all around the house, my father is a funk drummer, and my sister played piano and sang in the choirs at school. I remember having music playing a lot of the time, and having a blast watching my dad perform with his friends. I wasn't any different, and started piano and violin lessons as well as singing in the choirs at church and at school. When I got to high school, I started taking private voice lessons, and a very insightful teacher introduced me to opera. Looking back on it, it's pretty hilarious how skeptical I was about my ability to do it, but after a few years went by I got a scholarship to study opera in college, and the rest is history.

These days I have a successful performing career doing classical music concerts and the occasional opera all over the country, as well as teaching a handful of incredibly bright and talented young singers. In addition to that, I've found a correlative career in helping others plan their visions and it brings me so much joy. I finally feel like I'm stepping into the version of myself that I always wanted to be, and it really is amazing to be here. Given my background, it was inevitable that I would end up making music a big part of my life, and honestly, the people who know me best aren't surprised by the planning part either, but the road to how I got here is a long and winding one.

After I left college, I spent a few years studying music independently and working as an administrative assistant before deciding to go back to school. When my husband, who's also an opera singer, and I got married we managed to get into the same graduate school, so we packed up our bags and left Mesa, AZ for St. Louis, MO. Fast forward two years when I graduated and found that even though I learned some amazing stuff, I had all the wrong skills to thrive in the music industry.

When I began graduate school, I was full of hope and promise, mixed with a good sturdy dose of enthusiasm for what I thought would surely be an immediately successful career in classical music. I would love to tell you that's how it went, but it definitely did not. I completely and totally fell flat on my face trying to make it in the world of professional opera. I accepted my degree with a sense of fear, lack of confidence in my abilities, and very low self-worth, not to mention none of the essential skills it takes to be a successful musician in this day and age.

I quickly found myself not getting hired for music jobs, having no idea how to act like a professional, not having a clue how to get a job in the first place, and worst of all not singing nearly as well as I needed to if I wanted to make a living. Despite my fancy advanced degree and years of study, my self-esteem was completely shot. Watching some of my peers make strides in their music career while I felt like I was totally spinning my wheels made me feel terrible. After I totally bombed a competition because of my lack of technique, I almost gave up on the thing I loved to do most because I had no idea how to fix my problems and create a plan to make my goal a reality.

Fortunately for me, I attended a performance that totally changed my life. I saw a production of Turandot and was blown away by the leading soprano. She was captivating and her vocal technique was flawless

– the moment I saw her my passion was reignited and I said to myself "I need to learn to sing like that." I connected with her after the show, and she agreed to give me a voice lesson. About five minutes in my mind was totally blown, and she uncovered more sound than I thought I could make. She said to me, you need to call my teacher and work with her. When she gave me her information I about fell over: Carol Kirkpatrick was her teacher's name, and is someone I had sung for 3 or 4 years prior.

My dear reader, you know about Carol and how she changed my life by now, but please allow me to share a little more about what happened. She was well known in the industry as an exceptional mentor and expert in the business of singing, and I knew it had to be a sign that here she was right in front of me again. So, I contacted her and as I suspected she told me I was singing like crap. That I knew, but the thing that really stuck out to me was this: she said, "You are just throwing spaghetti at the wall and hoping for something to stick." She was right. I had no plan, no real discipline, and no consistency, let alone a strategy for how to make it happen. Worst of all, every day I was building a set of habits that were carrying me further and further away from my goal. After our conversation she took me under her wing, reconstructed my singing technique, taught me the importance of living my life on purpose so I could build a plan to reach my goals, and enjoy life every step of the way – bumps and all. I was finally allowed to be unapologetically myself.

That's how I wound up here. The more I stepped into myself the more I realized I had to give. When I started getting hired to sing consistently and thinking like a business person instead of a starving artist, my colleagues started coming to me for help. But most importantly, I had to develop the same habits of consistent focus and self-care that take elite athletes to the championship. I had to treat myself with respect and love. I had to show up. I had to be willing to look long and hard at myself and discover where I was holding myself back, how I could use my strengths to my advantage, and how to make my weaknesses work for me instead of against me. Then, I was finally able to take the leap of writing a new story for myself.

Soon after that people outside of the arts were seeking me out for advice on how to reach their goals and creatively troubleshoot their obstacles. That's when I realized that the skill sets and tools I built up to be a successful professional singer are the same skills that most people need to sharpen if they want to execute a plan in their own business. I took some time to really sit down and define what key areas made the most impact on my business, and I developed my signature system to help my fellow business owners and entrepreneurs do the same thing. Every vision needs a plan, and when it's in motion you can feel freer and more confident than ever, and live a more joyful life even with all the ups and downs that may come your way.

Some thoughts on habits and change. Change is hard. Changing habits is hard. Recognizing that you need to change some of your habits to get what you want is probably the hardest part. But it can be done. And it doesn't need to be perfect, in fact, more often than not the process is messy, a little scary, and full of ups and downs… steps forward and steps back… You can do it. The process will take the time that it takes, and for it to stick it must be done in a way that is uniquely you. All the while, you need to remember that you are still enough. You're still going to make it, and you will eventually be just fine.

Here is a question that comes up a lot…. How do I know if I need to change a habit or not? I think the answer lies in the results. Are you getting the results you want in life? I mean… are you really? Or are you just kinda sorta getting results sometimes? If you have a habit that is actually propelling you forward without steamrolling right over other people, then it is probably one of the good ones. You've likely learned how to tap into it and use it to your advantage so you can get what you want. On the flip side, if whatever you're doing is frustrating you, and every time you do it you beat yourself up a little bit for not having been or done something a certain way, and you notice that you are getting further and further away from what you want… then perhaps this is a habit or behavior that you need to toss right out the door. Clearly, it isn't serving you, and you don't want it around.

When this happens, the tough part is consciously AND unconsciously flipping that habit and behavior upside down so you can start cruising through life in the way you want to. Accomplish things the way you want. Make the kind of impact you want to. And do it all with ease, elegance, and a dash of sass.

There have been many times when I thought I needed to behave a certain way, because it was keeping me safe. For example, I used to be so scared of singing with my whole voice. I didn't want to stick out, or be heard, or make a mistake, or be noticed, or go against the grain. But after many years of doing that I realized that if I didn't start making noise… big noise… carefree noise… MY noise… I would never feel whole. I would never reach the people that I wanted to reach, and I would never truly feel like I lived.

So, I did the work. I dug deep into the mess that was me and my insecurities and fear and I figured out some crucial things. I learned how to quit procrastinating, quit avoiding showing up at 100%, and I started to let myself be seen and heard… imperfections and all. Was it hard? Yes. Was it scary at times? Yes. Did I sometimes want to go back into my shell? Absolutely yes. But every single time I get the job done, I can see what kind of impact it makes. Even if it's just one person who needs to hear me, I know I did what I needed to do. These days, I understand what it takes to let my gifts make their way to the exact right person in the exact right moment, and that is worth all the scariness that comes with flipping things upside down and getting closer to your best self. So, no matter how silly you think your uniqueness is, somewhere out there is a perfect match to receive what you have to offer. Go find her! Someone needs you.

Coming up in the next chapter, we'll move on to discuss how you can use your newfound superpowers and all your other strengths to set up a system that allows you to stay focused on the things that bring you joy and move you towards your goal. We'll uncover tools that help you stay consistent, and unstick you when old habits like procrastination and overwhelm creep in to throw you off your game.

Points of Reflection:

- *What are some of the things you feel are holding you back?*
- *Are there any people you look up to who share similar traits?*
- *How can you reframe those perceived weaknesses into strengths?*
- *Try this exercise:*
  1. *Write out something that you feel is a weakness, i.e. I get overwhelmed by details and find myself daydreaming instead when I should be handling my to-do list.*
  2. *What is the opposite of that? I.e. I get overwhelmed by details but love to create a big picture.*
  3. *What are all the advantages of that opposite? I.e. I can create a big picture so it's easy for me to build large scale plans and be a visionary leader.*
  4. *How can you find someone to support you? I.e. I can get my partner or friend to help me manage the details after I create the vision.*
- *Who could benefit from what this newfound strength is?*

CHAPTER 5

There's Nothing Wrong with You, But There Might Be Something Wrong with Your System

What is wrong with me? Why can't I get this right already? How many times have you asked yourself those questions lately? How many times have you asked that of yourself today? If I had to guess, it's probably come up a lot for you. I know this because I used to be like that too, always wondering why I kept messing things up, why I wasn't further along, why I couldn't finish this, that, or the other thing. But let me tell you - when someone finally looked at me and said, "No, no... you just need to do that this way instead of the other way," I could have cried tears of joy.

I probably did cry tears of joy along with some tears of frustration over all the years I spent assuming there was something wrong with me because I couldn't get what I was after. But what a beautiful thing it was to learn that after all the trial and error, there was nothing inherently wrong with me. I was not messing everything up, nor was I destined to be a tremendous failure. I just needed to make a couple of tiny changes to the way I was doing things, not necessarily who I was.

That changed my whole world. It gave me the gift of learning how to look at my approach to how I was executing tasks before diving right in with no strategy, and actually giving something time to get some traction before I went and changed it to something else. It gave me the confidence to look at something objectively instead of emotionally and saying, "Okay… what specifically about this approach didn't work, and how can I change it to make sure it does next time?" Once you begin doing that for yourself, you will make so much progress so much faster! So, let me reiterate - there is nothing wrong with you. You are wonderful and beautiful and unique. But the reason you aren't feeling totally in love with the way things are going for you right now might be because there is something wrong with your system and the way you are doing things, or because the system is out of alignment with what you really want. And that's okay, because we can fix it.

Let's look at a common example I hear from a lot of my clients: *I can't get my things organized and I can never find anything.* More often than not, by the time they come to me they've tried everything. So I ask them "What have you tried doing to get yourself organized?" Then they proceed to list dozens of ways they've moved their things around without ever mentioning what they even want. Then I ask…. "What does being organized mean to you? Describe a set up that looks beautiful, is functional, and is easy for you to maintain with your lifestyle." That's when the lightbulb goes on. You see, typically all the things they've tried are things they've read or heard about, but they never put them up against their own desires and the way their days naturally flow. That is how a system can get off the rails from the jump. If you build something that works for someone else without checking in to make sure it works for you, you will surely get frustrated by rebuilding it over and over again.

Let's look at an example from a previous chapter. If you are a person who gets bogged down by details, yet you buy yourself a planner that is full of boxes to fill in, and time slots that make you feel like you need to fill in every moment of your day with a minuscule activity, you will never use it because it will stress you out. Instead, find a planner full of inspirational questions that allow you to dream up a vision, with plenty of big blocks of time for your schedule. Work from the top down to construct your day, not the bottom up.

If you want to save yourself some time, start with the end in mind. Think about what you want the end result to be, and make sure you really fill that vision out. Keep it a touch realistic so it's in alignment with what can truly fit into your life, but don't be afraid to challenge and stretch yourself some. I am a big fan of big juicy goals that are a little bit scary. Once you see the picture of what you want the end to be, build a system that gets you to that. In the case of organizing your home office, for example, think about these kinds of things before you get started.

> How much time do you spend there?
> Do you need things to be easy to access or is storing them out of sight more important to you?
> Do piles make you crazy or do they not bother you at all?

Here is another important point to consider: Is there something deeper on your mind? This is a big one. I worked with one client who couldn't get past the organization section because she just didn't really feel worthy of running a business from home to begin with. We had to get that limiting belief cleared out before we could even begin to get the office organized. She was quite literally sabotaging herself with a stack of untidy files because she thought she had no business being in business.

You have to have the right system if you want to stay consistent. There is power in the process, and the sooner you embrace it the faster you will gain the momentum that propels you straight into the arms of what you want.

Here's another one of my favorite examples that illustrates how to build a system or develop a process. Learning how to sing. Singing is not what you think it is. Most people seem to fall into two schools of thought: One, people just kind of roll out of bed with tons of talent, and you're either a good singer or not. Or two, singing takes tons and tons of difficult work and you have to do all kinds of crazy things with your mouth position and breathe from your diaphragm and micro-manage every single little muscle to get it right. The truth is it's a little bit of both. But the important thing to remember is that for singing to really work right, you have to keep it very, very simple.

We all come into this world knowing how to sing and make noise. Think about it. Babies instinctively know how to relax their bodies to allow the perfect amount of air to come into their lungs so they can release a powerful cry that gets the attention of the adults in their lives so they can have their needs met. Now think back to what you were like as a child. Probably loud, right? Children run around the playground playing and yelling and singing and shouting and it's no big deal. No one worries about their voices being judged and no one is overthinking it at this age.

When we get a little older, all of a sudden we become very aware of the fact that people can hear us. Then we do all kinds of things to change and modify our voices so they're pleasant to listen to, use our inside voices more frequently so we're not too loud, and begin to focus on posture and sitting up straight so we only take shallow breaths into our chests instead. Try that right now. Take a couple of breaths, and take note of where you feel the air flowing. Is your chest moving up and down, or is your abdomen expanding and allowing the air to gently fill your torso?

For a singer, this can really complicate the process because we have taken muscles that used to work perfectly well and naturally understood how to make a sound, and consciously convinced them all to work against each other. Add in the fear of our voices being judged and you have a perfect recipe for getting right in your own way and blocking your body's ability to get into flow and create a powerful, free sound.

By the time I reached my late twenties, I had been taking voice lessons for years. At this point in my studies, I had put considerable time, energy, and money into my instrument and getting it to function well. Seriously, I was two degrees into this thing. I was committed and working very hard to get it right. Unfortunately, I still found that whenever I stepped into the practice room or onto the stage I would open my mouth and have no earthly idea if the sound I wanted to make was going to come out right or not. Can you imagine? That kind of stress of not being able to tap into my flow and allow my instrument to play with ease created so much anxiety around my performances that I contemplated throwing in the towel altogether.

Fortunately for me, Carol was able to untie all my emotional knots in our very first lesson. "Singing is simple, not easy." She would say. She very clearly and articulately broke down the steps of the vocal process in a way that no one had ever done for me before. I'll spare you the nitty-gritty of vocal pedagogy but essentially it comes down to this: Open your mouth. Breathe. Sing. Stop Singing. Here I was trying to lift this, and manage this and control this and hold that, and all it had done was knock me out of alignment with something I had instinctively known how to do since birth.

It was a great reminder that my body is made of muscles and to sing well all you have to do is follow the steps of the process, the same way an athlete would with her athletic technique. If you watch a professional tennis player, you can see them swing the racket the same way every time. Football players pull their arms back to throw a pass the same way every time. Gymnasts prep to run and fling themselves into the air the same way every time. When the technique is in alignment with a strong mindset and focus it typically works out just how you want it to. Sometimes it doesn't, if we make a little misstep somewhere or there are external factors at play, but the point is it makes it much easier to get up and do it again if you know exactly where you went wrong in the process.

This, my friends, is how we have to approach our daily lives as well. This is particularly critical for those of us who get all caught up in the unnecessary drama of over scheduling ourselves, not knowing how to efficiently plan our days, saying yes to too many things and getting overwhelmed, being inconsistent with our routines, and so on. Before you know it you will stray so far from what brings you joy that you'll forget how to get it back.

That is why it is so important to think of ways you can apply the concept of simplicity to your lives, even if you live a complicated lifestyle. Most things can be broken down into very simple steps that will keep you right on target and moving forward. This also allows you to overcome things like procrastination and other habits that can keep you stressed out. Keep it simple.

When you're simplifying things, it's extraordinarily important that you consider what you want. This will always guide you right back to where you feel at peace, and help you clear away the mental clutter and get back to basics. Even if your day is packed to the brim with activities, if you tune into what you want before you make that daily schedule, it will remind you why you're doing it in the first place, and everything that isn't under the umbrella of what you want at the highest level will gradually start to fall away.

Now, I understand that sometimes there are things we have to do in our day-to-day that we really don't love, wouldn't choose to do in a million years, and you can't just not do those things. For me, one of those things is sorting the mail, among a myriad of other admin duties.

As much as I dislike that chore, it's not going to sort itself and having a clean desk makes it worth it. I'm saying that if you allow yourself to keep even those tasks connected to your why then all of a sudden it feels much lighter because you aren't all caught up in internal angst about it.

Sometimes my clients come to me making the simplest things into something very complicated. Creating a schedule is another topic that comes up frequently. Many of the women I work with ask for guidance with a system that is typically constructed with no real end result in mind. It's usually overstuffed with more things than a person could possibly do in one day, combined with an underestimation of how long it takes to do something and an overestimation of available time. What happens if you operate this way? It doesn't take many days to feel completely burned out and frustrated at the end of each day because you were busy every second but somehow only accomplished one thing on your to-do list.

That does nothing but make us feel out of control and like we can't do anything right. It would be like saying you're going to make a big fancy home-cooked meal with multiple complicated gourmet courses in 15 minutes, when you haven't even gone to the grocery store. That is a system that is set up to make you fail from the beginning.

So, keep it simple. When you're creating your schedule, be it on a monthly, daily, or weekly basis - whatever feels good to you - ask yourself these questions:

> What do you want your day to look like?
> How do you want to feel at the end of your day?
> What is the one thing you must do that will make you feel like you won today?

That's it. That's all you get. And it really is that simple. From there, you can start to fill in appointments and add tasks, duties, chores, and other commitments, but if you frame it around what kind of day you want to create and how you want to feel when you get back into bed at night, it can really change everything. Even if your day goes totally off the rails and things come up that pull you away from your schedule, knowing that you left room for flexibility will make you feel like you are running your schedule instead of your schedule running you, and you can easily get back on track the next day.

Productivity is another hot topic. We are so obsessed with getting things done that we forget that being busy isn't the same as being productive. In fact, so many times busyness is the very thing that is keeping us from being productive in the first place.

Do you remember the last time you had a really awesome, super productive day? And I don't mean the kind of day where you got 129 tasks done, but I mean the kind of day where you actually moved the needle forward on your goals and dreams. The tasks you put your energy and effort into were things that moved you closer to where you wanted to be, and further closed the gap from where you are today. That kind of productive. That feeling where you could confidently look back and say, "I was awesome today, I DID that."

That sort of feeling is so incredible, and you can have it anytime. Really, you could only do one thing on your list and have it, as long as you did the right thing. But how do you figure that out? And how do you know if the items on your list are actually moving you forward or just keeping you stuck in dramatic busyness?

When it comes to getting things done, less is more. Once you focus in on what you want to do on a larger scale you can break it down into smaller, more manageable steps. Then, you can focus on one step at a time, giving it your very best, until it's complete. You will find that even if all the time you have to spare on it is 10 minutes a day, if those 10 minutes are spent truly giving your love to the task in front of you and being present in the moment, you will see yourself at the finish line much sooner than you envisioned.

And trust me, I hear you. What about all those little day-to-day tasks that must get done and suck up all my energy? There is a place for those too. But, before you go filling up your calendar with things like that, you must first sit down and ask yourself if they are things you really have to do. Here's a tool I like to employ when I'm having one of those days where it feels like I have a million things to do, and I can feel that overwhelming feeling of not knowing where to begin to creep up on me.

Stop, grab a piece of paper, and write every single thing down that you think you have to do. All of it. Personal, business, errands, large projects, tasks for your kids if you have them, etc. Just write it all out until it's all on the page. Some people like to do this electronically and if that's you go for it. I prefer the pen to paper method because something about it relaxes me, and the next step is even more satisfying. Once it's all on the paper, take a break. Give your brain some time to feel and relax into the empty space you just created. The next step will be easier when you have taken the time to rest, so give yourself permission to be still and trust that the rest is part of the task.

Once you're feeling the clarity come through, review your list and cross off anything that you don't really need to do, or at the very least what you don't really need to do right this second. This one can be hard because it feels like everything is important, but be honest with yourself - what can go? What can wait? What can you delegate to someone else? Once you've whittled your list down some, you can begin to rearrange it and prioritize with fewer things there to distract you, so you are only focusing on the things that you truly need to get done. This is how you design a to-do list that gives you the freedom to enjoy what matters most to you.

When you aren't mentally bogged down with too many things to do and a lack of clarity around how to get them done, you free yourself up to create, or build, or simply do. This is when you'll begin to feel free and focused. That will radiate out in the world as confidence, setting you up to help others while you're getting your own things done.

Coming up, we'll spend some time talking about two important words that can make or break your system. Flexibility and Failure. When you learn to master the first one, handling the second one becomes much easier.

Points of Reflection:

- *Are there any systems in your life that aren't quite working for you?*
- *How would you change them if you could?*
- *When you think about your natural strengths from chapter four, how can you factor that into building your system?*
- *In what ways might your system be sabotaging your productivity?*
- *What can you change that will make you feel like you're back on track?*

CHAPTER 6

Flexibility is Your Friend

ew Year's is my Christmas. I'm serious. Most people who celebrate it get all excited about hopping out of bed on Christmas morning to open their gifts, watch their kids have fun, and enjoy a big breakfast. Not me. While I do love Christmas and celebrate it with enthusiasm, my bolting-out-of-bed behavior is reserved for the week of the new year. There is just something about the energy of closing out one year and welcoming in another that fills me with so much joy and excitement that I can hardly contain myself. In fact, I tend to celebrate it in my own way for the days leading up to that midnight countdown and a couple days past it. Not always with drinking and parties, although some years that can be quite a fun choice, but for the rituals I've created around endings and beginnings.

I have several little things I like to do for myself, from making sure my house is clean, to writing those first words in my brand new, carefully selected planner. But the best are those moments I take to go somewhere quiet and reflect on the previous year by recounting what went well, what didn't, and expressing gratitude for it all. Next comes setting my intentions for the new year, aligning them with my business and personal goals, and bridging the gap by creating a plan of action based on what happened in the previous year.

I love this. I practically live for those moments of quiet solitude where I can get all up in my imagination and plan my future vision. The funny part is, nearly every time, the way I end the year looks nothing like the way I intended to begin it, with perhaps the exception of hitting those critical milestones and goals I set for myself. Even though the outcome is the same, the way I got there is usually full of some twists and turns and surprises. Many times, the outcome is even better than I thought it would be because of what happened along the way. That is why, whenever you make any kind of plan it needs to be rigid enough to keep you focused and on target, but flexible enough to regroup when things go off the rails so you can see other opportunities that are even better than the ones you dreamed up.

If you're a fan of cooking shows like I am, then you may have noticed that competitions are super hot right now. Inevitably there is an episode where some chef is in the throes of the competition, cruising along, feeling in the groove and just crushing things up against the clock and all that stress, when they pull out the final dish or critical element with half the time gone, only to find that it is a disaster. Not just a little disaster that can be covered up with some delicious Chantilly cream or a red wine reduction, but a complete and total unservable mess. Not at all what they wanted or set out to do in the beginning, and if it goes on the plate then they are surely out of the game they so badly wanted to win. Sometimes it's a total mystery as to why the recipe they've made a zillion times goes so wrong. Sometimes it is easy to figure out the problem and can be boiled down to an oven that cooks a little hot in the on-set kitchen. Other times, it's a risk with flavor or technique the chef took that just went horribly awry. Either way, this is not it. This is not the business and it will not do.

As viewers we all go through the same range of emotions those chefs are feeling at that moment, and can sometimes even imagine what we would do if we were in a kitchen staring down a ticking clock, holding a pot of curdled lemon curd with $10,000 on the line. Anyway, one of two things usually happens here. The chef, totally dejected, puts it on the plate and faces the judging table already defeated and just accepts that things didn't go his way this time. Or, the chef says "Not today lemon curd, you are gonna do what I tell you to do" and rallies to make some magnificent delicious second batch, or magically comes up with something even better just in the nick of time, thrills the judges' taste buds, and takes home the prize amid cheers and tears of joy. It's really pretty exhilarating, particularly the latter of those two options.

Now, what does this have to do with you? Quite a bit, actually, and particularly so in those moments where you come face to face with something that has not turned out the way you thought it would for one reason or another. And you too have two options. You can either a) just accept it, and keep on moving no matter what it costs you, or b) you can take a beat, reset, come up with a new plan, and see what kind of magic you can create for yourself. Of course, my personal preference here is option b, because no one should stay stuck in a situation that doesn't totally delight them just because they feel like they should. That will make you sad and cranky, and I'll say it again in case you missed it: if you are not happy and not walking through life giving us your best stuff because of it, you are doing a major disservice to the people you love who need your best stuff.

My schedule involves quite a bit of travel, and as you can imagine it does not always go according to plan. Delays, cancelations, crazy weather, cranky passengers, cramped accommodations, it all happens and can change the course of a trip at a moment's notice. I used to get incredibly stressed about travel, but over the years I've learned to change my attitude. I do my best to focus on the beautiful little moments of joy on every trip - meeting kind strangers, getting my favorite local treats, and making sure to connect with dear friends and family in each location does a lot to help me look forward to things. On top of that, building a little bit of my routine from home into each trip goes a long way to help me feel grounded away from home and move through the changes of environment with ease. I always expect the unexpected and know that I can only control so much. There is nothing I can do about the weather or a broken plane, and frankly, I would rather get to my destination safe but late than not at all.

One trip, in particular, tested every bit of my relaxed travel attitude and I had to embrace the concept of having a plan that is both flexible but concrete at the same time. I was heading from Denver, CO to Phoenix, AZ for a concert on Easter weekend. I was especially excited about this because my parents lived near Phoenix at the time, so I would get to see them and several beloved friends of our family. Springtime in Denver is notorious for big, heavy snow, so I knew I would need to keep an eye on the weather. Knowing that, I wasn't too worried when I saw a winter storm warning that coincided with the day of my flight, but nevertheless I decided to take some extra precautions.

I packed early and called the airline, asking if I could get on an earlier flight to get out ahead of the storm. There was a rehearsal on the evening of my arrival that I didn't want to miss. They assured me that it wasn't a problem, and my flight would likely be fine since it left so early in the morning. That was that, so I went on with my evening and got up early the next morning to make the trip to the airport. On my way, I noticed some drops of sleet starting to fall and went into my happy place to keep the faith that it would work out and I would get out of there. By the time I got to the airport, the sleet had turned to snow, and the snowfall had turned to a full-blown whiteout. It was coming down hard, and that heavy wet snow told all of us at the terminal that it was about to be a rough morning in the airport.

After making my way through security and up to the gate, I took a look at the airplane covered in snow and was not even a little bit surprised to see that our departure time had been delayed an hour. "No big deal," I thought. "I'll get some coffee, have some breakfast, and be on my way in an hour." Little did I know my airport adventure was just getting started.

About an hour later, they called us to board the plane. We all got settled in and ready for take-off, when the captain announced that the weather conditions were too bad and the tower would not let us take off because of it. So, rather than keep us all on a freezing plane rocking in the windy blizzard conditions, we all gathered our things and deboarded. At this point, we were all asking the gate agents if the flight would be canceled. If that had been the case, I could have rebooked my flight for the next day and gone back home before the storm got worse. Unfortunately, that is not what was in store for me. Not only did the airline not cancel the flight, they just continued to push out the delay for several more hours. At one point, the power even went out in the airport, which by the way is slightly terrifying, but the folks in charge were still adamant that we would take off.

You can probably guess what happened. After one more round of boarding, then deboarding because the power outage fried the de-icing machines needed to thaw the plane out, we did not take off. If that wasn't frustrating enough, the FAA had grounded all planes coming in and out of Denver because the storm was so bad. On top of that, there was a major accident on the freeway leading in and out of the airport, completely blocking traffic. Simply put, we were all stuck. No one was going anywhere, not even to their home a few miles away.

This is about when I knew if I wanted to make it to that concert, I would have to figure something out and figure it out quickly. I did my very best to stay calm, made some friends, and off we went to the gate agent to get rebooked. Now, if you've ever been trapped in an airport in a major storm then you know what this situation is like. I did not, and was completely unprepared for the throngs of people who also had someplace to be and no way to get there. Very quickly, I realized that I was going to have to get really creative, have a lot of faith and patience, and somehow keep my cool if I wanted this to work out. I got on the phone with the music director and let her know what had happened, then got on the phone with my dad to tell him the situation too. I put them in touch so they could see about a back-up plan, while I did my best to sweet talk customer service into helping me out.

A few hours, several lines, and dozens of phone calls later, I had a standby ticket booked for a flight the next morning on a different airline. It wasn't what I had hoped for, and certainly not what I had planned for, but it was the best we could do. My new airport friends and I grabbed some dinner and drinks, and tried to get as comfortable and warm as one can be sleeping on an airport floor. The next morning, I got up early and spent the entire day running from gate to gate to gate with about 30 other people hoping my name would be called for a coveted standby spot out of that airport. At one point, I was so tired and frustrated that I called my mom in tears, telling her I didn't know if it would ever work. She encouraged me to take a few deep breaths and stop running long enough to get some water and a snack, and keep trying. Thank God for moms, right? Eventually, the crowd thinned out and I got the glorious call from the gate agent that there was a spot on the next flight for me. I then flew from Denver, to Sacramento, to Phoenix, and somehow made it to Arizona in one piece, luggage and all.

So, my friend, it might not be quite as dramatic as being stranded in an airport for 36 hours on your way to a performance, but sooner or later in your life you will have a moment when your plans go so far off the rails that you will have no choice but to hunker down and buckle up for the ride. This journey towards self-discovery and owning that beautiful light of yours is no joke, and full of twists and turns. But if the goal is important enough to you, you will find a way to get to it, or redirect your attention to something that gives you an equal amount of joy instead of giving up entirely. When those surprise situations sneak up on you, here is what I would encourage you to do:

Get in the habit of practicing mental resilience. This takes work, but if you spend time every day looking at a challenging situation and finding a solution, it will get easier and easier to bounce back from the tough stuff. Particularly, if you do that deep work of believing that you really can do it you will find that it is easier to keep your cool in the toughest of situations. You begin to see that whatever happens, you can get a workable outcome even if the way you got there is nothing like you thought it would be. When you learn how to look for solutions and positivity even when things seem like they will never work out, suddenly even the most difficult problems don't seem so impossible.

When you are taking action, do so guided by your inspiration. Yes, you can create a plan, and yes you can put together an incredible system full of bells and whistles and well thought out steps - in fact, I encourage that kind of behavior because it's one of my favorite things. But when things start to go a little wild and you veer off course, listen to your gut to guide you back to the track. Remember what you are trying to accomplish and why you want it. Think about what kinds of things you do best and lead with those gifts. Lead with your light. In my adventure at the airport, my years working in customer service and the empathy I had for people working behind the counters because of it is what really helped me get on a flight that day. Every time I wanted to lose my cool, I listened to my intuition telling me to be kind. That as rough as my day was going, imagine what the airline staff were dealing with trying to get everyone to their destination. And so I was kind. I smiled when I felt like shouting, and offered compassionate conversation instead of making demands. It worked in my favor after several lovely people worked hard to get me out, and thanked me for my patience.

Now, let's unpack another topic that can throw us off course, and fast. Failure. What do you do when you fail so spectacularly that there is nothing else to be done but start over? I used to have a sweet and spicy cat named Silvio. He was precious, my little baby, and honestly, I'm still that woman who sits and pines for her dearly departed kitty even though he's been gone for years. What can I say, he was my first pet as an adult and I loved him. Silvio loved his breakfast. Specifically, he loved having it at around 5:30 am every day regardless of what kind of timeline my husband and I were on in the morning.

Silvio would do this thing where he'd go through a series of slightly annoying tasks to try and get one of us up to feed him. It started simple enough with him wiggling and rustling about in bed, making sure his bell moved so we could hear it. If that didn't work, he would jump down and run around a bit. If that didn't work, he would run faster, bolting across the bed and us. If that didn't work, he would start to deploy more aggressive tools. He would hop on top of a nightstand and swat one or two things down. We learned pretty quickly to keep the nightstand clear of swattable objects that tipped over easily, and that was that.

Next, he taught himself how to hop up on the dresser and bat at the picture frames - he loved this one and knew it was a baller move because he would just sit up there cool as can be, staring at us with his big green eyes all full of sass, and reach up there slowly with one paw to try and knock the picture down. It worked for a while, until we wised up and blocked the dresser so he couldn't get to the pictures in the first place. His big grand final move was to back up to the wall, run at the open bedroom door (all you pet people out there know that it saves loads of trouble if you leave your door open so the cat can come and go a million times at night) and launch - yes launch - his little cat body through the air and at the door so he could slam it shut with a cat version of a karate flying kick, thus startling us half to death and waking us up. This one was actually pretty impressive. But even then, once we caught on, we just added a doorstop so he couldn't do that anymore.

My point is, he was relentless. If something didn't work, or stopped working, he would figure something else out because one way or another, he was getting that breakfast. That is how I need you to be too when things don't work out the way you want them to or think they should the first time. Failure is an inevitable part of life, and life is far too short to sit around pouting and giving up because something didn't work. Your job is to look at it objectively for a moment, assess what didn't work, and then come up with a new strategy.

Do you have a right to feel your feelings? Absolutely yes! In fact, I encourage it. If this is something you put your heart and soul into then yes, of course, you are fully allowed to be sad, upset, disappointed, or whatever else comes up for you. We are all under a lot of pressure to "keep our heads up", or put on a brave face when the going gets rough, and while I appreciate that, if you don't fully process your feelings you'll be carrying around that baggage for way too long, and you won't truly be able to learn from your mistakes and grow past them. It is okay to feel your feelings. Yes, keep your vibe high, look for teachable moments, but remember that this process is full of ups and downs and you're going to need to give yourself some grace. Sometimes you just need to feel sad or overwhelmed or afraid for a few minutes. But then figure out why you feel that way, challenge those negative limiting beliefs popping up telling you that you aren't worth it or you can't do it or whatever, and move that vibe right back on up so you can get to work and keep sharing your gifts. Acknowledge those feelings, spend some time with them, and then once they've run their course, get right back at it and find a way to make it work. Failing at a thing does not make you a failure. It says nothing about you as a person, and definitely says nothing about your worth. It simply means that the thing didn't work this time, so you have some adjustments to make. Treat the failure as feedback, and give yourself enough grace to not take it so personally. I promise if you shift your perspective here you will feel so much better about really going for it, and not giving a flying cat what anybody thinks of you during the process, whether the outcome is a smashing success or not.

But what happens if you start to notice that you seem to be constantly messing things up in the same ways, when it comes to the same things, and never quite get the results you want? Here is the part where you have to look a little bit deeper and see if you are actually standing right in your own way. Self-sabotage is a peculiar concept because why would anybody purposely sabotage themselves and try to ruin the results? Why would someone try to not have the thing they want to have? As it turns out, fear of failure and fear of success are pretty closely related. After all, with great success comes great responsibility, and with greater responsibility comes the possibility that you'll fall even harder. So, sometimes our brains do this thing to us where in trying to protect us, they will cause us to stop instead of moving forward, or make a mistake we know better than making, all in the name of protecting us. Because deep down in there, somewhere we might fail, even if the failure happens after the success. And to our reptilian brains that is a very scary, threatening concept. No one wants to fail, or be perceived as a failure, or look like a fool in front of the people we love. Sometimes it's just easier to cut to the chase and make sure it all goes sideways before we even get close to that.

If you start to notice, hmmmm, this is a thing I seem to do over and over, whether it's procrastinating on a project you know would bring in income, or "forgetting" to get your bag ready the night before so you don't have to rush out of the door all stressed out the next morning, it is time to sit down and look at what is really going on. Is this behavior pattern causing a problem for you? If it is, what is the hidden reward? If on either side of the coin your brain recognizes a possible negative outcome, you are going to stay stuck right where you are. But here's the good thing: once you notice it's a problem, and notice how it's keeping you stuck, you can start to take action on transforming it into something amazing. From there you can move past it, and finally start to achieve the goals you have set for yourself so you can get to that big beautiful thing that is the life you desire for yourself. And all the while, you'll do it with panache and enjoy every step of the way, ups and downs included.

As we move toward the final parts of the book and methods I teach my clients, we'll discuss perhaps the most important topics of all. The concept of rest and self-care, and how important they are for your journey. In the following pages we'll cover some options you can use in your life to make sure you take the time to keep your cup full and your light shining brightly.

Points of Reflection:

- *What are some places in your life where you could be a little more flexible?*
- *Do you find it easy to be flexible? If so, why?*
- *Does being more flexible scare you? If so, why?*
- *What resonates with you more - fear of failure or fear of success?*
- *What are some ways you can find support when things don't go your way?*

CHAPTER 7

Never Underestimate the Power of Rest

There are some things you can't rush. Have you ever tasted a really good cake? Not just a cake that is simply delicious and enjoyable, but a cake that makes you stop and pause to take a breath. You get it in your mouth and on your tongue and have to take a second to savor the texture, and speculate about what's in there that is making it so exquisite. That kind of cake. There is this incredible pound cake recipe that the women in my family have been baking for decades. It is one of those very serious Southern cakes that requires way too many eggs and way too much butter, and you aren't allowed to have the recipe until you're GROWN grown. I didn't get it until I got married. My mother used to bake this cake for special occasions only, since it was rather elaborate for a pound cake, so I knew when I saw her assembling the ingredients that something wonderfully fun was going to happen sometime soon.

Who was it for? Was she taking it to someone? Would we get to eat it? Was it a holiday? And the holy grail for my little attention-loving self - was company coming over?! Sometimes I would get the answer and sometimes I wouldn't, but one thing was always certain: over the next few hours I was going to have to be quiet and wait.

You see, there's an old wives' tale that if you make too much noise in the house while you have a cake baking in the oven, your cake will fall. "Shhhhh, be quiet! You're going to make my cake fall!" is a refrain I am very familiar with, as I would often run through the kitchen from the backyard while my mother had something delicious baking away. Honestly, I don't really remember if the threat of a less than perfect cake did anything at all to get me to hush, you'll have to ask her, but it did stick with me. As I got older and started doing my own baking, I learned that it's not so much the sound that threatens to make the cake fall, but more like the vibrations disturbing the environment and causing fluctuations in temperature. That's less important now that we mostly use gas or electric ovens rather than coal stoves, but you get my point. If things started to get uneven while the ingredients were changing from batter to cake, something wouldn't work properly, and it would sink in the middle. Similarly, if the cake was taken out too early, or the temperature was wrong to begin with, it wouldn't rise the way it was supposed to.

This journey to transformation has some similarities. Here, as you do the work to become your favorite self, you are both the baker and the cake. You get to create a beautiful recipe that reflects all your desires and hopes and dreams, do all the mixing and the flavoring to get it just the way you want it, and then continue taking action on the things you can control and allow the process to take the time that it takes. Sometimes you'll feel like the impatient kid sitting on the floor trying to be quiet while she stares through the oven window, hoping that the cake stays in your house instead of going into some pretty packaging for a neighbor or a picnic. Other times you will simply need to stop. Many times, the real magic happens when you slow down to rest and wait, much like waiting for things to come together like a cake in the oven. That cannot be rushed or tampered with.

That step may be the hardest. When it's you that has to stop doing and just *be*, either because something still needs to shift inside you, or because you need to take some time to rest and grow stronger so you can begin to *do*, you must honor that and give it time. There is no need to rush your recovery, in fact, you should honor that time to slow down and heal. When you do, you learn how to take care of yourself so you can keep your cup filled no matter what. Don't resist it with a bunch of noise and disrupt the process. Get yourself somewhere calm, surround yourself with people who make you feel safe and cherished, and rest. This is not a race, it is your process alone. When it's time to move back into action, you will know.

When I work with my clients, a big part of our time together is uncovering some ways they can build excellent self-care routines into their daily lives, along with options for what to do when they feel a big need to stop things entirely for a moment. Here are some of our favorites.

Morning Routines

In the personal and professional development world, there is a lot of buzz surrounding the concept of morning routines. You hear from all sorts of people who get up at 4:00 am to work out, read, say their affirmations, etc. I too love a morning routine, and there is plenty of science out there that says the effects of setting up your day with a great routine is one of the fastest ways to see big returns on the things you are working to create. When you begin your day with intention and surround it with activities that support that intention, you will see a great improvement in how you move through the day, and what you accomplish. I admit, morning routines are something that I struggle with because I would rather stay up late. But the days that I follow through with my routine are the days that I feel the best by bedtime - no matter what has happened. Here are some activities you can choose from to add to your morning routine.

- Meditation or prayer
- Physical activity

- Journaling
- Reading
- Eating a nutritious breakfast
- Enjoying a cup of coffee or tea
- Doing something creative
- Breathwork
- Showering and getting ready for your day
- Doing the most important task on your to-do list

I could go on and on here, and really what you do in your morning routine is up to you as long as it leaves you feeling focused, energized, and full of the feelings you want to carry with you throughout the rest of the day.

Evening Routines

Have you ever woken up frantically trying to find what you need to get out of the door on time? If you have, you know how stressed out that can make you feel. That is why I firmly believe a solid morning routine begins in the evening. If you set up your evening to end with calm and structure, you will sleep better and be more likely to wake up with less stress and move easily into your morning routine. After you do both routines for several days in a row, you will train your mind to build these habits, and eventually begin moving through them on autopilot. Consider adding these to your evening routine.

- Reviewing what you completed that day
- Setting up your calendar and tasks for the upcoming day
- Writing in a gratitude journal
- Setting out your bag for the next day
- Getting the next day's lunches and breakfast ready for you and/or your family

- Spending time connecting with your family
- Reading
- Writing
- Doing a creative activity

You might notice that some of the tasks fall into both the morning and evening routine category. That's because it really is up to you and how these things make you feel. All of these are interchangeable, so feel free to be creative with how you construct your routines. If working out at night makes you feel ready to end the day, wonderful! If starting your day by reviewing the previous day helps you focus, excellent! This is all totally personal and customizable, so build it to your liking until it feels just right.

You might notice that I did not include things like checking social media or email. That's because those types of activities can pull your focus away from your own needs and into the needs of others. Think about it. How do you feel when you start scrolling through the news, or your social media feed? Do you notice any stress? Does a touch of overwhelm creep in? Pay attention to the cues your body gives you here, and if it is anything less than energized positivity it has no place in the routines that shape your day.

Playtime and Creative Outlets

I probably don't need to tell you that art and creativity are integral to my life. I could go on and on about how important it is for your productivity levels to give yourself a break by getting into your right brain periodically, but instead, I would rather just talk about fun. Remember how much fun we used to have as kids at recess? Those breaks in the day to run and play games and use our imaginations to make up stuff were some of my favorite times in life. Growing up in Arizona, we didn't see a lot of rain, so on the rare days that a storm kept us inside during recess I relished the time I could spend drawing, painting, or working on an art project. When you build in time to do something creative and fun, you will start to find that you have more energy on the other side of it. These are some of the activities my clients and I love:

- Cross Stitch
- Making handmade cards
- Playing an instrument
- Watercolors
- Creative Writing
- Playing games with your kids
- Playing with pets
- Coloring
- Painting
- Baking and cooking

The list of things to choose from here is endless. So, go explore and have fun. It's the perfect time to pick up that old hobby that you never got around to finishing. Whatever you decide, keep it light, have fun, and release any pressure you have on yourself to be perfect. That isn't what this is about. When you channel your playful inner child the results that show up in your adult life will not disappoint you.

Rest

Let's talk about actual, physical rest for a moment. I don't necessarily mean sleep here, although that's important too. Sometimes the answer to a problem really is to just find a way to take a nap. In this case, I mean taking time to pause in between activities so you can train yourself to be present on what you are focusing on instead of what you just did or what you need to do next. If you watch elite athletes before high stakes games or tournaments, you can see them tuning out everything around them and getting mentally into the zone. Sometimes you'll catch them listening to music, other times they sit in silence. But the theme is the same: they are still. In a moment of restful contemplation, preparing themselves for the upcoming task. This is something you can do too, and I encourage you to build moments of pause into your day. If you don't have the means to bookend your tasks with full-blown 15 minute breaks that's okay. Five minutes will do, and with practice, you can reset in thirty seconds.

There are many other factors that contribute to making sure your cup is full so you can keep growing and staying productive. Another critical element is having support. Get the support you need to make sure you are eating nutritious food and taking care of your physical and mental health. Find a network of people you love so your social interactions are meaningful and fulfilling. Take time to get out in nature, and discover ways to get in tune with your spirituality if that's important to you. This is all about you, and the rewards of taking excellent care of yourself will come back to you and your family in ways you never dreamed possible.

So, what happens when you need to halt everything entirely to take care of yourself and get your head and heart around a major shift? Every so often I'll have a moment where I'll just need to stop everything, and I mean everything. My autoresponders go on, text messages have to wait, food gets delivered, and I just hole up in my house and alternate between watching movies and napping. This is usually after a long stretch of "over extraverting" as my husband calls it, when I have attended event after event after event, and even my social butterfly self has had enough. I'm getting better at planning ahead and building these types of days into my schedule, but occasionally something will happen that knocks me on my tail seemingly out of the blue. In these cases, it's usually because something in my awareness has bumped up against a place where I am doing some growth. It's almost like when a caterpillar knows it's time to go into a cocoon for a while so he can change into a butterfly. There is nothing to be done but wait and rest.

These hibernation spells are not always fun either, and don't fit into the typical thoughts of self-care with mani-pedi's, chocolate, and wine. This is more like, deep soul searching, journaling, and sometimes lots of tears. In those really big transitional moments in my life, it felt like I have had to completely and totally undo something, shed a part of myself, and leave it behind, in order to get to the next thing that I wanted. This is similar to the caterpillar's journey too. Before they even get to the cocoon part, they grow and grow and shed their skin several times, and then when they get into their little cocoon they have to completely dissolve and rebuild their structure into that of a butterfly. It's amazing, and a process that cannot be rushed.

I spent about twelve years of my life chemically straightening my hair. Before video hair tutorials were easy to find and products for naturally curly African American hair were readily attainable, many of us just opted for straight, easier to manage hair. But something happened in the early 2000s. We started to see many Black women making the choice to embrace the natural texture of our hair and learn how to be creative with it. Haircare products started hitting the shelves, and video after video began to hit the internet with instructions for how to do anything from cleanse and moisturize, to detangle, to craft elaborate updos. It was exciting and inspiring, and a little bit scary too.

After years of back and forth, I decided that it was time for me to stop straightening my own hair and figure out how to manage these curls of mine. I got some opinions from my sister, who had been rocking her curls for decades and was way ahead of the times, as well as my hairdresser whom I trusted dearly. I had a few options. I could let my natural hair grow out, and trim the straight ends of my just-past-shoulder-length hair little by little. Or, I could do what's called The Big Chop. It's exactly what it sounds like, cutting off nearly all your hair to reveal a short curly pixie cut, or what's affectionately known as a Teeny Weenie Afro amongst Black women.

I figured, why take the slow route, and had worn my hair in a short style before so I opted to take it all off at once. When I looked in the mirror, I felt liberated and terrified all at once. I felt beautiful and empowered, but I had no idea how to take care of the fabulous curls that were finally making themselves seen. And so, there was nothing I could do but wait, let them grow in at their own pace, and learn how to keep them healthy. Sometimes it was frustrating and sometimes it was amazing, but eventually I got comfortable with the fact that this was a process that would take the time it would take, and I may as well get comfortable and enjoy it.

Whatever it is that you are resting for, I encourage you to enjoy the time and teach yourself not to get impatient. When the time comes to get back to work, you will be more ready than ever before and the results will be extraordinary.

In the final chapter, we'll explore the concepts of gratitude and relationships. Together, we'll look at some of the ways your transformation will open you up to approaching life from a place of gratitude, and how you can use this as an opportunity to connect with people more deeply. This part of the process is where you will begin to bring your light to the world even brighter than before and step so far into it that others will want to join you.

Points of Reflection:

- *What activities will you build into your morning routine?*
- *What activities will you build into your evening routine?*
- *What creative activities have you always wanted to try?*
- *Where can you find time to enjoy some rest and quiet?*

CHAPTER 8

Gratitude Makes You Stronger

*B*e grateful for the little moments. Be grateful for the small joys and the big wins. That deep, all-encompassing feeling of gratitude is one of my favorite feelings to surrender to because it brings me such a sense of peace. Be grateful for the lessons. There is wisdom in them, and they will help you refocus and get back on track, even for the hard parts of this journey. Sometimes, it's hard to see what to be grateful for until some time has passed, hindsight is 2020 after all. But if you can get into the habit of being grateful for whatever is happening to you right now, in this moment, and forgive yourself for those choices and decisions you made that pulled you off track, you will move in and out of all of this with much more ease. When you get knocked out of your light, you can get up, dust yourself off, and jump right back in it when you get into the habit of saying "Whoops, thanks for the stumble… now I understand why that happened."

One of the hardest and most painful lessons I've ever had to learn was that sometimes for something wonderful to show up you have to let go of something else.

We never really had pets growing up. Aside from a guinea pig I had in elementary school, we were pretty much a pet-free house. Not for any real reason, we all loved animals. Owning a larger pet just wasn't something my family chose to do. My husband, on the other hand, grew up in a household full of pets. Cats, dogs, guinea pigs, tortoises, birds, lizards - you name it, at one point he and his family had one. So, naturally, after we got married, one of the first things he said to me after we settled into our new graduate student life in a new city was, "I think it's time to grow our family. Let's get a cat."

Now, I was slightly allergic to cats, didn't know anything about them, and really had no idea why we should even consider trying to take care of one while we were in grad school. My husband knew better though, and with the help of our friend who worked at an animal shelter, convinced me to take a trip down there to "go play with the kittens." Of course, I got totally played. They both knew that the second I snuggled a little soft kitten I would be hooked, and they were right.

Some folks think that the animal actually chooses you, and now I fully buy into that perspective. In this busy shelter full of meowing kittens, I was drawn to a cage inhabited by a little gray fluff ball with the biggest ears on him that I'd ever seen on a cat. He was tired and groggy from a little eye infection he was recovering from, and so couldn't hang out in the playroom with the other cats. I asked to hold him, and he wasted no time before cuddling up and falling asleep on me. Given my love of naps on a soft surface, I knew this cat was coming home with me.

Silvio became one of the great loves of my life. He was full of sass and drama that was fitting of a cat with two opera singer parents, and wanted nothing more than to eat, sleep, and toss mildly judgemental looks my way from time to time. He never minded when I practiced, in fact, would usually come out to sit under the piano or on top of the bookshelf while I did so, and would always run to meet me at the door when I came home. He was the best napping buddy, and without fail would come when I called him. This cat had it figured out - my husband was for feeding and playtime, and I was for love and care.

We discovered pretty early on that Silvio had a little heart murmur that was most pronounced when he was stressed, and that we would have to monitor it for his whole life. A few months after he turned eight years old, I noticed that he was a little extra tired and had begun napping in places he didn't usually pass out in. I didn't think much of it because his eating habits hadn't changed and he was otherwise fine. But what I didn't know was that my time with my sweet baby cat was coming to an end.

One night we were watching a movie and just doing our little family thing like we normally did. Silvio was asleep in my lap. He hopped up to go eat and wandered off into the bedroom. After a few minutes went by, I heard him start to howl. I had gotten to know his cries pretty good at this point and knew when he was sick or scared or just being fussy, or wanted food or attention or whatever. But this one was different. I had never heard this noise before, so my husband and I jumped up and ran to find him. There he was, curled up in a little ball, howling with fear and the most awful look on his face. I got down on the floor with him to take a closer look, when he got up and sort of hobbled to the bathroom and laid his little body on the tile. He was still howling, and at that point had begun panting... and I knew. My little baby was in pain and something was not right.

I hollered at my husband to call the emergency vet because Silvio was sick. I scooped him up into a carrier and rushed him to the animal hospital, riding with him in the back seat. If you've ever had a cat go through some pain, let me tell you... the noise they make is horrible and hearing it from him was breaking my heart. About 15 minutes after this all began, he was in the care of the vet. When she came out to the waiting room, only a few minutes later, I could tell by the look on her face that it was not going to be good news.

"Your cat has gone into congestive heart failure and has kicked out three blood clots, cutting off the circulation in three of his legs."

Saddle thrombosis. An excruciatingly painful condition for a cat, and a cat owner's nightmare. I asked her what the treatment was while I pulled out my credit card. I didn't care how much it cost, I just wanted my cat to live and feel better. She rattled off a list of tests, medications, procedures, and potential surgeries that he would need, emphasizing that the biggest concern was getting him to survive the night given the major possibility that another clot could escape at any moment. She also said that in the months following stabilization and treatment, the odds were very high that this would happen again. She made it clear that this was one of the most severe cases she had ever seen.

I was stunned. I didn't know what to do, and I was completely unprepared for the emotions that overtake you when you face the decision of what to do with a sick or injured pet. Even my husband, who had lost dozens of pets, was visibly emotional about this one. I asked the vet what she would do if she were me. She responded by saying that she had three cats and loved them like her children. But in her professional opinion, my cat's case was so bad that the treatment would be even harder on him, and he would never be the same. She insisted that it was my decision, but if it were her and her cat, she would let him go.

I sat with that for a few moments and contemplated how I could just give up and not try to help him heal. How I should give him a chance to fight. Mind you, it had only been about 25 minutes at this point so I had not been afforded the opportunity to process any of this. Even so, I knew in my gut that as much as I wanted him to stay, that wouldn't be good for him. He hated his vet appointments when he was healthy, and putting him through dozens of tests and appointments would be a terrible existence for him. I would be keeping him around for my sake, and that wasn't fair.

So, we went back to the exam room with the vet and prepared to say goodbye to my little man for the last time. When she brought him in, he was still howling, indicating that the pain meds were barely working.

My husband scooped him up and I sat by his head so he could see me when he left, and he just looked at me with the biggest eyes, almost begging me to let him go so the pain would stop. That's when I knew I was making the right choice.

I would love to say that I moved through this situation with grace, but I would be lying. Putting my cat to sleep so suddenly absolutely wrecked me for a long time. I missed him so much and didn't know how I would recover from the loss, while at the same time feeling incredibly foolish because it was just a cat and I could go get another one whenever I felt like it. But as time passed, something amazing began to happen. Not only did I start to heal, but some opportunities began to present themselves that wouldn't have been possible to take if I had a pet. My out of town engagements started picking up, taking me on the road more often. My husband and I moved across the country and found the perfect home to rent… that didn't allow pets. I began to realize that Silvio left me at the perfect moment. His passing happened at a time when things were slow enough to lean into my grief and fully experience it, while making way for new opportunities to present themselves soon after that I may not have been open to otherwise.

As painful and traumatic as this was, it was the perfect lesson in how to let go of something in order to allow yourself to move forward and embrace what is truly meant for you in this life. I am a person who makes spirituality a daily practice, and chose to believe that on some level, Silvio's little soul knew this. He knew his job was done here on earth and it was time for him to go so I could grow. I am incredibly grateful for that experience, and frequently think of it when I'm faced with another difficult decision when I need to let go of something in order to make room for something new. Sometimes it's painful, sometimes it's not, but it always works out in the end. Eventually, I can take the time to marinate in my gratitude and thank whatever it was for being a presence in my life at the time. Sometimes it's easier to see when it's time to release some things more than others, but now I know to lean into the gratitude of the lesson and trust that it's happening at just the right time.

Expressing gratitude doesn't always have to look like this or come with pain and trauma. Back in the day, I used to work a lot of retail. It always appealed to me, and I was actually pretty good at some parts of it, particularly helping customers on the floor. I got to meet all kinds of women, help them figure out what kind of style suited them best, and get them all dressed up. In the process, I would often get to know them a little bit and we'd have a fun time bonding over sheath dresses and blazers. One year I had to work a short shift on my birthday. It wasn't really a big deal; there were only four short hours between me and my celebration, so I wasn't bothered by it. I tried to be cool and not go on and on about myself because let me tell you… I love my birthday. I treat myself for the whole month and I'm not even ashamed.

And you know what else I love? Gifts. If you're familiar with the Five Love Languages by Dr. Gary Chapman, he talks about how receiving gifts is a major way people give and receive love. That is for sure my love language. I love everything about gifts. Getting them. Giving them. Surprising people with random presents. Spending hours choosing the perfect shiny wrapping paper and creating a perfect little beautiful package. It rarely even matters what the gift is to me. I mean obviously I take extra delight in a really thoughtful perfectly selected present, but seriously, you could wrap up a toothpick for me and I would lose my mind over the cute bow and tiny box. I don't know what it is, but there you have it.

So here I am, working on my birthday smiling like the Cheshire Cat because I'm having a silent party for myself in my head, and counting the minutes until I could head to my favorite store and buy myself a present - and yes, have them gift wrap it for me because that is a thing I do - when in come these two women. They are laughing and hollering and kind of carrying on, and I immediately knew I would have an amazing time helping these women shop. I moved closer to them as they made their way through the store and noticed that one of them had on some kind of big sparkling crown, buttons, and a sash. Was this a bachelorette celebration? Oh no. The second the women came up to me the decked out one shouted:

"It's my Birthday!!!!!"

I hadn't even gotten out my "Hello there, welcome" before she was alerting me of her special day, dressed in enough flair to make sure everyone knew she was celebrating herself. I, of course, thought the whole thing was glorious. Once we stopped clapping and cheering, I told her that guess what, it was my birthday too! Now, this sent both of us into a bit of a frenzy. I had met my birthday twin who was equally excited about her own celebration as I was about mine. There was some bouncing up and down, a big hug, and a few "Woo Hoos!!!!" before she stopped dead in her tracks, looked me in the eye and said with complete seriousness, "Why are you working on your birthday?" It was like I was committing some kind of crime. She looked legit horrified at the thought of it. I reassured her that it was a very short shift, and soon I would be gallivanting through the mall and celebrating for the rest of the day. Her face melted with relief, then we went on with our shopping spree and I showed her all my favorite items in the store.

After an hour or so, I walked her to the register and we said our goodbyes. I went back to my smiling and straightening hangers, very pleased at the super fun birthday twin experience I just had. About 15 minutes later, my new friend came back into the store shouting my name. I looked up, and as she was making a beeline straight for me, I noticed that she was carrying something in her hand. She came up to me and handed me the biggest, most beautiful arrangement of a chocolate-covered strawberry bouquet I had ever seen and said, "Thank you for a wonderful experience, these are for you. I wanted to make sure you had a special sweet treat on your birthday. Happy Birthday!"

We hugged again, whooped and hollered one more time, I said thank you several times and we parted ways. As soon as she was gone, I went straight to the office and completely lost it. I mean ugly happy tears y'all. My manager probably thought I was nuts. This woman, this stranger, had taken the time out of her celebration and spent her own money to get me a present just to make sure I had an extra special day. And in the process, she expressed her thanks for helping her pick out some nice things. I was completely undone and blown away by her generosity. This was the gift I didn't even know I needed, and to this day it is the best gift I have ever received from anyone.

You see, that's the thing about gifts. You never know what kind of impact they are truly having on another person. This woman's generosity, enthusiasm, and unabashed ability to be so loud and proud about celebrating herself had brought me more joy than I had experienced on a birthday in a long time. She shared a part of herself with me that I am still moved and inspired by, and was fearless in doing so.

We all have gifts that are inside of us, and could make an impact on someone's life if we had the courage to share them. Is it possible that for a second that woman thought to herself, "Maybe I shouldn't, maybe she'll think I'm a weirdo." Of course. But even if she hesitated, I'll never know because she did it anyway, and I'm forever changed by that beautiful moment. And have been inspired to give more surprise gifts ever since. So, if you have a gift that you aren't sure if you should share, please stop hesitating and give it away fearlessly. There is someone out there who needs it, and who will be deeply affected by it. You have the power to change someone's life and the lives of many others, and they will be grateful for you.

So, how has the concept of practicing more gratitude shaped my relationships? Interestingly enough, it has transformed them in a way that I didn't know was possible. This is because, when we show up leading with gratitude, we begin to be grateful for our relationships with the people we are interacting with. This begins to shift something in our behavior that allows us to put the needs of others at the forefront of the interaction, and make sure that we are making them feel cared for and appreciated.

Imagine what your life would be like if every time someone crossed your path, you were so grateful for them, and showed so much care for them that you made them feel like they were on top of the world? And imagine if people treated you the same way, and made you feel like a special part of their lives just for existing? Gratitude is so powerful, and when you infuse it into the way you treat others, the ripple of positivity is astounding.

Something else begins to happen as well. When you are taking care of others because you are so grateful for them and love them so much, sometimes you find some inner strength to stand up for them and yourself in ways you didn't know you could. I know many women who still believe that they should be seen and not heard, shouldn't raise their voices, challenge others, or speak their truth. Sometimes, you will be called to do this in a way that you feel unprepared for, but if you can rise to the challenge and approach it with grace and gratitude for the lesson, you will experience incredible growth.

I'm not a person who yells. Generally, if there is a conflict, I do my very best to remain calm and level-headed and resolve it by asking questions that deescalate the situation. Particularly if I'm in a position of mediating a conflict between other people. This has been my preferred method for years, even in the cases where a little extra oomph would have likely helped, for instance in corporate settings where I am working with male leaders who occasionally interrupt me or disregard my opinion and expertise.

Recently, I had been feeling the pull to stand up for myself more and state my opinion with confidence instead of worrying that what I had to say would cause more conflict. Sure enough, the perfect opportunity to practice this new skill dropped right into my lap in the form of a consulting contract for a small business development firm. Right from the beginning, I knew the owner was going to be a challenging person to work with, and that my suggestions for improving his organization's systems and infrastructure would not be taken seriously, nevertheless, I continued so I could lean a little further out of my comfort zone.

Have you ever worked with someone who was just... difficult? I'm sure you have at some point or another. The leader of this company was very, very difficult. He would flip his personality back and forth on a dime to become extraordinarily charming, only to fly off the handle in a rage at any moment. Frankly, it was exhausting to be around, and I could see how this was creating problems for his team.

One day I was in a meeting with him and three other employees. We were going through what should have been the very simple process of laying out the steps of a new workflow template. However, we had barely gotten started when the leader began to lose his temper and started yelling at the guys on his team for asking perfectly reasonable questions. You see, he felt that everyone should be reading his mind and know what he wanted, so the clarifying questions they were asking set him off pretty quickly. I looked around the room and could see how frustrated this made the guys because it was clearly something they had to put up with all the time, and was not only tanking the morale of the company but was also ruining productivity. It was at this point that I attempted to step in and de-escalate things so we could get back to work and end the meeting on time.

"Why don't we all take a short break," I said, before asking the owner to step into the hallway with me for a brief conversation. To my surprise, he shouted "No, anything you have to say to me you can say in front of them. If I'm being an asshole, tell me to my face."

I was stunned. No one had ever spoken to me like that in a professional setting, and I knew that my usual method of playing it cool was not going to get the job done with this man. So, I took a couple of deep breaths, gathered my thoughts as quickly as I could before looking this grown man dead in the eye and saying firmly and clearly, "Okay, if this is how you want to do this then let's do it. You are being an asshole. We are meeting about a very simple process and need you to articulate your wishes in a way that ensures anyone can execute the plan for you. This should be simple, fun, and move very quickly. However, your temper is ruining this meeting, and your behavior is completely and totally unacceptable. Either get it together so we can move on, or we are tabling this until another day."

This was SO hard for me. I have never, ever had to speak to the Executive Director of a company that way, and I had no idea what his reaction would be. Not only was it totally not my style to be so aggressive in my communication, even though it was what I was feeling and knew was right, but I had no idea how this unpredictable personality would react. I sat there for a moment in silence, just letting the tension hang in the air. I looked around the conference table and saw a look on the face of each team member that was a combination of relief and disbelief that told me no one had had the courage to stand up to him the way I did before. When I looked back at the boss, he was slumped over in his seat, pouting like an actual child. After a minute or two of silence, he muttered something under his breath, and to my surprise, completely and totally changed his demeanor. He didn't apologize, mind you, but he did immediately lighten up the mood with some humor that broke the tension and made the space for us to have a productive meeting that went smoothly and ended on time.

Afterward, all the guys thanked me for doing what they had always needed someone to do: speak the truth they could not speak and advocate for their best interests. I was pretty relieved that it turned out so well, and also incredibly proud of myself for doing something that felt so uncomfortable to me. The best part about it was that I was able to stand up and speak in a way that while challenging for me, was still in alignment with who I am. I didn't yell or lose my temper, I was calm but firm, and I found a strength I didn't even know I had. The fact that my courage had led to others being grateful for me was the icing on the cake.

The lesson here is this: sooner or later, you will be called to stand up and dig into your power because you are in a situation that can only be healed by your doing so. It may be scary, it may be unexpected. But it is something you must do to help facilitate your own growth which will ripple out to positively affect everyone you connect with. Be grateful for the lesson. Be grateful for your strength. Treat others as if you are so grateful for them and their best interests that you not stepping up would be doing them a disservice. Do this with respect and love, and watch the people in your world rise to meet your new standard, then bask in the glow of the light you are radiating out to the world. It's time for you to shine.

Points of Reflection:

- *What is a tough lesson you've learned to be grateful for?*
- *How can you practice gratitude more in your life?*
- *What are some things you can do to express gratitude for others?*
- *How will you practice approaching your relationships with a sense of gratitude?*
- *What ways do you think gratitude will help you handle challenging situations?*

Afterword

When I sat down to start this book, I did what I usually do and imagined what I wanted the end of the journey to look like and how I wanted to feel when I completed the project. I anticipated that it would be a long process full of ups and downs, which it was. I also thought that the end result would probably be different than I thought it would be when I began, which has also proven to be true. However, what I didn't anticipate was when it came time to do the final edits and write this afterword, the entire world would have changed in a drastic way.

Right now, countries all over the world are facing a global pandemic. A new coronavirus, also known as COVID-19 began to appear a few months ago and has taken over with rapid ferocity. Governments everywhere are closing their country's borders and pleading with citizens to stay at home as much as possible, all in an effort to contain the spread of the deadly virus and keep hospitals from running out of supplies. I returned home from a month-long trip on March 10th, to promptly get my things in order, shop for groceries, and prepare to shelter in place for the unforeseeable future.

This is not at all the environment I had planned to wrap up this book in. I had been looking forward to fun launch parties, more travel to share and introduce this project to my friends and colleagues, and making an impact by sharing my own light with as many people as possible. Instead, I'm at home discovering that now more than ever, is the time for me to take my own advice.

You see, the effects of this virus have been monumental, and unprecedented in our lifetime. Closures of schools have turned the education system upside down. Businesses have closed, causing waves of unemployment and financial uncertainty. The arts and entertainment industry has taken a tremendous hit with concerts and events closed indefinitely. People are stressed, afraid, anxious, and unsure of how to cope with all the changes. Not knowing when things will improve, or what our new normal will look like when they do, is making it hard for all of us to go on about business as usual.

For me, I am finding that it's crucial to take this time away from the things I became used to and to go back through the L.I.G.H.T Formula for myself. After all, If I'm not going full speed ahead on projects and plans, I don't feel useful. And right now, it's hard, even for me, to stay motivated and keep up with my routines since there is nowhere for me to go. It seems like rest is the order of the day, and giving myself grace when I need to recharge my anxious batteries is the only thing that will help me stay sane during all the uncertainty.

I don't know what things will be like in the world when you read this book. But I do know that now, more than ever, we need every bit of light that we can muster. Working together to stay connected, to continue to inspire each other, and to bring our best to the table – whatever that happens to be at the time – is critical right now, and always. That is why my work is so important. That is what will keep me moving forward as we navigate these uncharted waters as a society.

I encourage you to review all the steps in the L.I.G.H.T. Formula and the Points of Reflection Questions frequently. That is really the heart of what I hoped to convey with the words in this book. No matter what is happening in the world, I want you to be able to tap into all the beautiful things that make you wonderful. When you get knocked down a bit, I want you to have the tools to pick yourself up again and keep moving forward. I want you to have the strength to show up and shine even when things get dark. Because those are the times when it's most important for you to do so. And when you fully find your joy and move through these tools with confidence and ease, I cannot wait for you to experience that moment again and again. Just imagine what kind of world we would live in if we all dared to shine so bright.

So, my friend, I hope you enjoyed my words, and that you feel more empowered to put them into action. Thank you for taking the time to read my story, and I look forward to seeing the effects of what happens when you become your favorite self, and own your light.

Acknowledgements

There are so many wonderful people in my world who have helped me do what I never dreamed I would do and write a book. First, to all the music and voice teachers I have ever had, thank you from the bottom of my heart. I wouldn't be able to do any of the things I've done in this life without any of you. Most notably, Lois Garrett, thank you for seeing that spark in me and nurturing it for so many years. Deborah Raymond, thank you for fanning those little flames into a fire. Carol Kirkpatrick, thank you for demanding that I never let that flame burn out.

To my Industry Rockstar family and coaches, thank you for truly getting me and everything that I'm about, and for all of the support you've given me on each phase of this crazy entrepreneurial journey. Extra special shout outs to Jen Graffice - the best acountabilabuddy there is, Greg Storkan - the only person on the planet who can make me dissolve into tears of laughter, and Jeremy Sutton - who has shown me the beauty of being the random minor note.

To my wonderful writing coach Samantha Worthington, thank you for your incredible guidance and support throughout every step of this process.

To my students and clients, who inspire me every second and teach me how to show up as my favorite self each day.

My dear Ball family (Mom, Dad, and Erica and Mike) and Sitzler family (Dennis & Darlene, Jeff, Jen, Addy & Aden, and Dan, Aimee, Poppy & Winnie), I know this book comes to most of you as a surprise, so thank you for allowing me to keep this project a secret! I love you all so very much!

I have been fortunate to have some incredible friendships, but thank you Erin Baize, Marva Whitaker, Bryan Hall, Jay Chacon, Joshua Zabatta, Erika LaForest, Brad Rogers, and Marcos Vigil for being in this journey of life with me for the long haul.

To my husband Tom Sitzler - thank you for all that you are, and for always enthusiastically putting up with my projects. I love you.

And finally, thank you dear reader for spending some time with me here in these pages. I hope my words have helped you find your inner light, stand in it proudly, and beam it out for all to see.

About the Author

Stephanie Ann Ball's journey into classical voice began at a young age when her parents introduced her to many different types of music. Her father, a funk drummer, taught her about popular forms of music, while her mother gave her more of the classical and gospel musical experience. She was a performer from the get-go, and found her niche when she began studying voice in high school. Her journey into the opera world began as an undergraduate at Northern Arizona University, and she continued her studies at Washington University in St. Louis where she received a Master's Degree in Vocal Performance.

Following graduate school, Stephanie realized that there was a tremendous gap between what she wanted to accomplish and what she was actually accomplishing. This discovery set her on the path to learn as much as she could about personal development and strategic implementation, as well as how to use her inherent strengths to her advantage. Using a unique approach to high performance she calls The L.I.G.H.T. Formula, Stephanie combines her background in the arts with her adept knowledge of sales, customer service, and administrative support to help her clients achieve extraordinary results when it comes to reaching their goals and getting themselves organized. Additionally, Stephanie is a certified NLP practitioner and has quickly become one of the most in-demand high performance consultants in the nation.

She maintains an active performance career. Stephanie has become a favorite of opera and oratorio-loving audiences across the country and has won many prestigious awards, including district winner of the Metropolitan Opera National Council Auditions in both Arizona and Kansas City.

As a highly sought-after concert artist and curator, she has performed on stages alongside world-renowned composers. Stephanie has been invited to perform as a guest artist on concert series' across the United States. In recent years, she has created three concept programs that showcase the many contributions African Americans have made to classical music. Passionate about sharing the joy of classical music and its benefits with new listeners, Stephanie continually makes an effort to introduce opera to her community and has done educational outreach with several companies across the country.

Own Your Light is Stephanie's first book. Now residing in Philadelphia, PA, she can be found obsessing over pastries and miniature desserts, browsing for bunnies on animal rescue sites, or wandering around an office supply store.

Connect with Stephanie

Stephanie resides in Philadelphia and has fully embraced her entrepreneurial spark. She loves helping her clients get a clear picture of where they are so they can raise the bar on their level of performance and achieve the results they desire, allowing them to truly show up as their best for the people they love most. Additionally, her signature concert series' have brought joy and excitement to companies all over the country.

To purchase her assessment and discover more about how to use the L.I.G.H.T. Formula, visit www.stephanieannballconsulting.com/light-formula

To learn more about how you can work with her,
visit: www.stephanieannballconsulting.com/work-with-me

To learn more about how to book her for your next event,
visit: www.stephanieannballconsulting.com/speaking

To contact Stephanie, visit: www.stephanieannballconsulting.com/contact

To follow her singing career,
visit www.stephanieannball.com

Find her on social media:
Facebook
https://www.facebook.com/StephABall/
and https://www.facebook.com/StephanieAnnBallSoprano/

Instagram and Twitter
@iamstephaball

LinkedIn
https://www.linkedin.com/in/iamstephaball/